DOCTO
THE GR

C000319513

DOCTOR WHO AND
THE GREEN DEATH

Based on the BBC television serial by
Robert Sloman by arrangement with the
British Broadcasting Corporation

MALCOLM HULKE

Illustrated by Alan Willow

A TARGET BOOK
published by
the Paperback Division of
W. H. Allen & Co. Ltd

A Target Book
Published in 1975
by the Paperback Division of
W. H. Allen & Co. Ltd
A Howard & Wyndham Company
44 Hill Street, London W1X 8LB

Reprinted 1979
Reprinted 1982

Printed in Great Britain

ISBN 0 426 11543 0

Contents

'Wealth in Our Time!'

In his forty years as a coal miner Ted Hughes had never
seen anything like it. He stood in one of the deserted
mine's main galleries, not believing his eyes . . .

Llanfairfach Colliery, in a mountainous part of
Wales, had been closed for some time. No one in the
village saw the sense of this – particularly the miners
who had spent their lives hewing coal from the pit.
There was still ample coal down there, enough for
another hundred years of mining. But government economists in London had 'proved' it was better business to buy
oil overseas than to mine coal here in Britain. So, Llanfairfach's coal mine had been closed and its miners put out
of work. But just in case it should ever be needed again,
a handful of older miners were kept on to make monthly
inspections. Today it had been Ted Hughes's turn to put
on the traditional helmet with its miner's lamp, and to
descend alone the 500 yards into the mine . . .

The inspection followed a set pattern. He walked along
one gallery after another, checking the props that held
up the roof, checking water levels where water seeped in,
pausing from time to time to listen. Sometimes he would
hear a faint creaking sound – the mine talking, as he
and his mates called it. If the sound was soft and gentle,
like a woman murmuring in sleep, the mine was safe.
But if the sound was ever harsh and sharp, it warned of
danger, and the possibility of a gallery roof collapsing.
In his forty years as a miner, Ted had known four major
roof collapses; men had been crushed to death or left

trapped to die of suffocation. And the minor accidents – chunks of rock falling from the roof, breaking an arm or leg, injuries which left a man crippled for life – were too numerous to remember.

After two hours of walking the galleries and checking the props, Ted sat down for a ten-minute break. He had a thermos flask of tea and some cheese sandwiches that his wife had made for him. As he poured himself some tea the old sadness came over him. He looked up and down the section of gallery where he was sitting, thinking back on the old times when the mine had been worked and was full of his friends. There was no one to talk to now. Economists in London had made a calculation, and the friendly world of Ted Hughes had been brought to an end.

He finished his sandwiches and was just about to start on the next part of the inspection when he noticed the green phosphorescent glow. It was coming from the far end of the gallery.

There is no natural light in a mine. The only light is artificial, and comes either from bulbs along the galleries or the lamps on the helmets of the miners. Ted's first reaction, therefore, was that he was no longer alone.

'Hello,' he called, 'who's down there?'

Pleased at the prospect of human company, he walked down the gallery towards the green glow. Then it struck him as odd that anyone should bring a *green* light into a coal mine.

'Hello?' he called again, pausing this time. 'Who's down there?'

Again no answer, but this time a faint bubbling sound.

Ted hurried forward. He still could not see the source of the light. It was apparently round a corner of the gallery, and he was eager to know what caused it. If anyone had been given permission to come down into the mine, Ted should have been told. But he couldn't think of a reason why anyone would want to.

Finally Ted reached the corner of the gallery, and then he saw it. Green glowing sludge was pouring in from a crack in the roof, cascading down a wall and forming a pool on the floor. The pool of sludge was already two or three inches thick in some places, and it bubbled as though alive.

Ted moved forward cautiously. Instinctively he wanted to touch it, but common sense told him to keep his distance. He backed away. Then, as he turned to go, a crack appeared in the ceiling above him. He looked up in time to see green sludge start to pour through from above. Before he had time to jump out of the way, a droplet of sludge landed on his left trouser leg. Without thinking, he tried to brush it off. The sludge stuck to his fingers and he could feel it bite into the skin. He rubbed them against the rocky wall of the mine. The surplus sludge went from his fingers on to the wall. But the parts of his fingers that had touched the sludge now glowed green.

He raced along the gallery towards the mine's lift shaft. When he got to the lift, panting for breath, he looked at his fingers in horror. The whole of his hand was now glowing bright green. He fell into the colliery lift, slammed the gates, and pulled the lever that would hurtle him 500 yards up to the surface.

While the village of Llanfairfach had lost its coal mine, it had gained Panorama Chemicals. This was a new industry in the village, with a small oil refinery, very modern office buildings, and an imposing set of gates and high fences to keep out intruders.

A large number of villagers were gathered outside the main gates when Dr Thomas Stevens, managing director of Panorama Chemicals, arrived in his big black chauffeur-driven car. As the gates opened to admit the car, angry fists waved at Dr Stevens and a number of posters were held out in front of him. They read 'Free

His fingers now glowed green . . .

Wales', 'English Out!', and 'Jobs for Coal Miners'. The elegantly dressed Dr Stevens smiled back at everyone through the glass windows of his vast limousine, and the car glided forward to the front entrance of the main administration block. Mark Elgin, the company's public relations officer, was standing there to greet Dr Stevens. Elgin opened the car's door, and Dr Stevens stepped out.

'Welcome back, sir,' said Elgin. 'What's the news?'

'It's all good,' said Dr Stevens. Then he gestured to the crowd on the other side of the main gate. 'How long has this been going on?'

'Since early this morning,' said Elgin. 'The usual unemployed layabouts.' Elgin came from a working-class background himself, but through being bright at examinations had gone to university, and now considered himself superior to others less fortunate.

Dr Stevens, who was feeling in a slightly more benevolent mood, put on a show of concern for the people crowded on the other side of the gate. 'But what's worrying them this time?' he asked.

'I suppose, sir,' said Elgin, 'they want to know what is going to happen.'

'In that case,' replied Dr Stevens, 'I shall tell them.' He went forward to the gate so that the people could hear him, and waved a piece of paper at them. 'I have here in my hand,' he said slowly and loudly, 'a paper which will mean a great deal to all of you.' He paused for dramatic effect, then called out: 'Wealth in our time!'

A small cheer went up from some members of the village crowd. Dr Stevens took a couple of steps nearer to the gates.

'Of course we all regret that the National Coal Board closed down the mine,' he said, not regretting it at all himself but knowing this would please his listeners. 'But we must not be bitter. We have to face facts. Coal is a dying industry. Oil is our future now, and the Government agrees with me. They have not only given us the go-ahead for our plans – they have promised us money for expansion. I have it here in black and white.' He waved the paper again. Actually it was the menu from the hotel where he had stopped off to have lunch, but he knew no one could get near enough to read it. He really did have a letter from the Government in his brief case in the car but he couldn't be bothered to fetch it. 'This means money for all of us. More jobs, more houses, more cars.'

A tall young man shouted something in Welsh. He had a tousled head of black hair, blue jeans and a polo neck sweater, and stood out from the crowd.

Dr Stevens smiled, as he had been taught to smile at his minor public school when he couldn't understand something. 'I'm terribly sorry,' he said, 'but I haven't mastered your language yet.'

'Then I'll repeat it in English,' shouted the young man. 'What you're offering means more muck, more devastation, and more death.'

Elgin sidled up beside Dr Stevens and spoke quietly. 'That's Professor Jones. He's a trouble maker.'

'If he's *the* Professor Jones,' said Dr Stevens, 'he is also a Nobel Prize winner.' Dr Stevens was always impressed with success because he was a snob.

'Because of that Nobel Prize,' said Elgin, 'he gets his name in the newspapers a lot. I suggest, sir, you go easy with him.'

Dr Stevens nodded, then raised his voice again to the crowd. 'It seems that some do not agree with my vision of the future. But there are always those who resist progress.'

'You call it progress?' shouted Professor Jones. He turned to the villagers. 'Don't listen to him. He's only interested in fatter profits for Panorama Chemicals at the expense of your land, the air you breathe, and the health of your kids.'

Dai Evans, one of the older villagers, spoke up. 'It's

12

all right for you,' he shouted at the young professor. 'You can afford to live the way you want to. We need jobs. We don't want to live on nuts.'

The crowd laughed. In Llanfairfach, young Professor Jones was respected but not accepted. To be accepted you had to have three generations of dead behind you in the village graveyard; above all, both you and they had to be miners. Professor Clifford Jones had come to the village only two years ago. He and some friends had bought a big old house where they set up The Wholeweal Community. They lived together communally, refused to own motor cars and would eat only natural foods. Thus they carried out a living protest against pollution and the destruction by industry of our natural environment. The villagers recognised the good intentions of The Wholeweal Community, but couldn't help joking about them. Their house was known locally as The Nut Hatch because the Wholewealers were believed to eat nuts instead of meat.

Professor Jones went red in the face at Dai Evans's remark. He earnestly wanted to help the villagers – to help everybody – and it threw him off his stroke when they were too ignorant to understand him. He replied in a stream of Welsh.

Morgan the milkman cut in sharply: 'For goodness' sake, man, stop talking Welsh with that stupid Cardiff accent. You only learnt it out of a book. You know half of us have forgotten how to speak it.'

'Then more's the pity,' said Professor Jones. He turned to Dai Evans. 'I'm surprised with you, Dai Evans. Of course you need a job – it's every man's right to have work. But there should be a coal mine for you to work in, not a chemicals factory!'

'I'm facing facts,' replied Dai Evans. 'The Government says coal is finished. It's oil now.'

Professor Jones asked, 'Were you facing facts when you went on strike for seven months?'

13

Dai Evans blushed and everyone went quiet. The memory of the General Strike in 1926 was still with many of them. For seven bitter months the coal miners had remained on strike until finally they were defeated because they had no food.

'I was only a boy in those days,' said Dai Evans quietly, remembering the humiliation of the miners' defeat. 'I learnt that sometimes you have to give in.'

'Even if it means you are being exploited?' asked Professor Jones.

'The workers have always had bosses,' said Dai Evans, 'people who live off our backs, so we might as well accept that. It's all right for you to tell us what to do, boyo, with your university education. But we're simple people, and none of us has got himself tens of thousands of pounds winning a Nobel Prize – '

Dai Evans stopped mid-sentence. From the direction of the mine they all heard the wail of the pit head siren. It could mean only one thing – a disaster in the mine. Without another thought the crowd of villagers turned and ran towards the closed mine.

'There's no one down there,' said Professor Jones as he ran beside Dai Evans. 'How can there be an accident?'

'There was Ted Hughes went down for an inspection this morning,' Dai Evans answered, panting to keep up with the younger man.

The first villager to reach the mine was Bert Pritchard, in his fifties but lithe and wiry as a whippet. He went straight into the pit head office. Whoever had pulled the siren lever must be in there. He came out at once, his face white, and his hands raised to the crowd.

'Maybe the professor should come in here,' he shouted. 'He might be able to understand it.'

Professor Jones pushed his way forward. 'What is it?'

'See for yourself,' said Bert Pritchard.

Professor Jones entered the office, followed by Dai Evans and Bert Pritchard. Ted Hughes was seated there, his hand still on the siren lever as he had pulled it. By his stillness and staring eyes they knew he was dead.

His hands and face and neck were glowing bright green.

2

The Doctor Plans a Holiday

In the Doctor's laboratory at UNIT Headquarters Jo
was reading the morning newspaper, eating an apple,
and occasionally looking up to see what the Doctor was
doing. The door of the TARDIS was open and the
Doctor kept popping in and out making adjustments to
an electrical circuit unit. After a while Jo asked:

'What *are* you trying to do?'

The Doctor, about to enter the TARDIS again,
paused. 'I'm not *trying* to do anything. I'm doing it.'

'Great,' said Jo. 'But what is it?'

'I'm preparing the TARDIS to travel to Metebelis
Three.'

Jo asked, 'Whatever for?'

'I thought we could do with a little holiday,' said the
Doctor. 'It's a particularly beautiful planet. Everything is
blue, even its sun.'

'What if you're needed here?' said Jo. 'Have you asked
the Brigadier's permission to take leave?'

'My dear Jo,' said the Doctor, 'I'm not bound hand
and foot to UNIT. I'm the scientific adviser, not a clerk.
I am free to go and come as I please.'

'Provided you can make the TARDIS actually go anywhere,' retorted Jo. 'I thought the Time Lords decided
where it could go?'

The Doctor looked quite affronted. 'I admit there have
been occasional problems, but this time I shall be in complete control. Metebelis Three is somewhere I've always
wanted to show you –'

But Jo wasn't listening. Something in the newspaper had caught her eye. 'Listen to this,' she said indignantly, and read from the newspaper: ' "The Ministry has at last given the green light to Panorama Chemicals." '

The Doctor completely misunderstood Jo's sudden interruption of his train of thought. 'Not a green light,' he said, 'a blue light. The sky is blue, the ground is blue. They even have some very pretty blue birds there . . .'

But Jo was equally absorbed. 'Listen to this bit,' she said, and read from the newspaper again: ' "Commonsense has triumphed at last".' She threw down the paper. 'Don't the Government realise the pollution that'll be caused if Panorama Chemicals goes ahead?'

'Also,' the Doctor went on, 'they have some very beautiful blue sapphires, and I hope to get hold of one.'

'Were you listening to me?' asked Jo.

'You seem to have gone off at a tangent,' said the Doctor.

'I'm going to do more than that,' said Jo. 'I'm going to go off at a . . . Well, I mean I'm going to pack a suitcase.'

'What a good idea,' approved the Doctor. 'I should have the TARDIS ready to leave in a few minutes.'

'The TARDIS?' said Jo. 'Oh no, I mean that I'm going to this place in Wales, Llanfairfach.'

The Doctor looked astounded. 'Whatever for?'

'Why don't you read the newspaper sometimes?' said Jo, making for the door. 'Then you'd know what for.' She stormed out.

The Doctor carefully put down the electrical circuit unit and picked up the discarded newspaper. He was just beginning to read about the Government's decision to support Panorama Chemicals when the Brigadier came in.

'Morning, Doctor,' he called chirpily. 'Reading the newspaper, I see.'

'How very observant of you,' said the Doctor.

17

'Well,' said the Brigadier, 'I've got a very interesting little job for you. Chap in Wales came up from a mine glowing bright green. Think you might be able to find out why?'

'Why what?' asked the Doctor.

'Why he's glowing bright green,' said the Brigadier. 'Bit odd, don't you think?'

'Has anyone tried asking him?' said the Doctor.

The Brigadier put on his solemn expression, reserved for State occasions and military funerals. 'The poor fellow is dead.'

'Surely that's something for the police,' said the Doctor. 'We're not policemen.'

The Brigadier lowered his voice, even though no one could possibly be listening to their conversation. 'Between you and me, Doctor, there may be international implications. Possibility of sabotage at Panorama Chemicals.'

'It's all I keep hearing about this morning,' protested the Doctor, 'this firm called Panorama Chemicals.'

'Big stuff,' said the Brigadier. 'Important connections at high levels. UNIT's duty is to protect them. My duty.'

'Then do your duty, Brigadier,' said the Doctor. 'Play at being a policeman if you wish.'

Jo entered wearing a raincoat and carrying a small suitcase. 'I think I left my newspaper,' she said.

'Where are you off to?' asked the Brigadier.

'Wales,' answered Jo, taking her newspaper from the Doctor. 'To do something about Panorama Chemicals before it kills us all.'

'My dear young woman,' said the Brigadier, 'may I remind you that you are a member of UNIT, and I have just received orders to *protect* Panorama Chemicals – '

'Then you'd better issue an order for my arrest,' Jo cut in. 'Fling me into a dungeon, have me court martialled.' She made for the door.

The Brigadier turned to the Doctor for help. 'Doctor, please, tell her she must remain here.'

'She works for you,' said the Doctor, 'not me.'

The Brigadier appealed to Jo. 'Miss Grant, you could at least explain what you have in mind!'

'I could,' she said, 'but I don't think you would understand. Our stupid Government has told Panorama Chemicals that they can go ahead with their plans to try and manufacture oil artificially. The result could be universal pollution. There's a man called Professor Clifford Jones who's fighting against Panorama Chemicals. He needs all the support he can get. So I'm going to help him.'

'I've heard of that man,' said the Brigadier. 'He's an impractical dreamer.'

Jo tucked the newspaper neatly under her arm, ready to go. 'So, sir, were Jesus of Nazareth, Christopher Columbus, and Marconi.'

The Brigadier studied Jo for a moment, then smiled. 'Well, perhaps we can discuss this on the way.'

'What do you mean, sir?'

'I have to go there too,' said the Brigadier. 'My mission is rather different from yours, but you could at least accept a lift.' He turned back to the Doctor. 'I hope you will be coming along as well, Doctor.'

The Doctor was preoccupied with his electrical circuit unit. 'Sorry, Brigadier. I'm not a policeman, and I *am* going to Metebelis Three. Miss Grant can explain to you where that is on your little jaunt.'

'I see.' The Brigadier's face was grim. He was not used to his orders being disobeyed. He returned his attention to Jo. 'Well, Miss Grant, I'll meet you in the car park in ten minutes.' He stalked out, ignoring the Doctor.

'Tell me,' said the Doctor, 'why are you really going to this place?'

'Because I've read so much about Professor Jones. He's fighting for everything that's important – the sort of things you've always fought for.' Jo paused. 'In a way he reminds me of a . . . well, a younger you.'

'I don't know whether to feel flattered or insulted,' said the Doctor, smiling. 'But don't worry. I do understand.' He moved over to the TARDIS. 'I hope he lives up to your expectations.'

'Doctor,' said Jo, suddenly apprehensive, 'you will be coming back from this Metebelis place?'

'After I've had a little holiday,' he said. 'Sure you wouldn't like to come along? According to the Time Lords' files there are no monsters, only a few friendly animals. The weather is always fine, and beautiful blue flowers grow in profusion.'

She shook her head. 'My place is here on Earth, Doctor. Have a good trip.'

The Doctor entered the TARDIS, then looked out from the door. 'Tell the Brigadier I'll follow you both down to Wales later.'

Jo beamed. 'That's marvellous!'

But the Doctor had already closed the door. Almost immediately Jo heard the sound of the TARDIS dematerialising, like the trumpeting of a thousand wild elephants. Then, as she watched, the battered old police box slowly disappeared.

Two million light years away the little planet called Metebelis Three slowly orbited its huge blue sun. No space traveller had landed there in three hundred thousand years since a lone Time Lord stayed for a few hours and wrote up the report that was later filed by the Time Lords.

The silence of a valley of blue rock was suddenly broken by the arrival of the TARDIS. Using hyperdrive, passing through Time and space, the TARDIS had travelled the two million light years in nil-time. Inside the TARDIS the Doctor made his usual checks of external atmosphere, gravity, and the possible presence of harmful radiation. The dials and meters on his console proved that in the previous three hundred thousand years, nothing had changed. Metebelis Three was as safe and inviting as it had always been. Through a monitor screen set over the console, the Doctor was able to look out onto the valley. He saw a bed of huge blue flowers growing quite close to where the TARDIS had landed. A bright blue butterfly had just settled on one of the flowers.

Looking forward to his holiday on the little planet, the Doctor opened the door and stepped out. His particular quest was to find the blue sapphires for which the planet was famous. These, according to the Time Lords' files, were at the top of a mountain not far from this particular valley. He closed the door of the TARDIS behind him, locked it and pocketed the key. Then he strode over to take a closer look at the flowers and the butterfly.

As the Doctor approached the flowers they turned their heads towards him, as though in greeting. Then their petals opened to the full, and from inside each flower came a venomous hissing sound. The butterfly rose up and flew straight at the Doctor's face. Droplets of venom struck the Doctor's hands and face, stinging him. Alarmed, the Doctor stepped back. A ground plant with straggling blue tentacles wrapped itself around his right ankle. As he dragged his foot away, three enormous blue birds swept down at him from the sky, squawking and trying to nip at his face with their blue beaks. The Doctor raised his hands to fight them off. One of the birds bit his finger.

From further down the valley came the pounding of hooves. He turned to see a herd of blue unicorns bearing down upon him.

The Doctor ran for his life, pursued by blue birds, blue unicorns, and spat at with venom by blue flowers.

His holiday was not turning out quite as he had hoped.

3

Land of My Fathers

The Brigadier pulled on the handbrake of his jeep. 'I trust two weeks will give you enough time to do whatever it is you want, Miss Grant?' They had stopped outside a rambling old farmhouse on the edge of the village of Llanfairfach. Over the door of the house were painted with loving care the words 'WELCOME TO WHOLE-WEAL.' With less loving care someone else had chalked on the wall of the house 'THE NUT HATCH', and 'NUTTERS GO BACK TO CARDIFF'.

Jo reached into the back of the jeep for her suitcase. 'I've no idea, sir. It depends how much Professor Jones needs help.'

'You realise,' said the Brigadier, 'that I ought to put you on a charge for dereliction of duty? However, while you were busy saying goodbye to the Doctor, I checked your file. You have two weeks' leave owing to you.'

'Thank you very much,' said Jo, getting out of the jeep. 'I'll bear that in mind.'

The Brigadier looked at the big old house. 'Bit run down, don't you think? Windows haven't been cleaned in months.'

'Then that's something I can do to help,' said Jo pertly.

'The place probably needs re-plumbing and re-wiring,' the Brigadier went on, amusing himself at Jo's expense. 'Still, I suppose you know best.'

'I can survive without luxury,' said Jo, although looking at the house she began to wonder what it might be like inside. 'There haven't been any grand hotels in my work with the Doctor, you know.'

'Oh well,' said the Brigadier. 'If you get fed up with the Wholeweal Community, you know where to find me. Over at Panorama Chemicals.'

'On the other side,' said Jo.

'Unlike you, Miss Grant, I have an open mind about Panorama Chemicals.'

'There are times, sir,' said Jo, 'when I think you have an open mind about everything.'

'Meaning I have no opinions?'

'Meaning,' said Jo politely, 'that it's important to have opinions, and to stick to them.'

'I suspect,' said the Brigadier, letting out the handbrake, 'that this conversation is verging on insubordination.' He smiled to show he meant no harm. 'Best of luck.'

'Thank you, sir.' Jo suddenly remembered the important thing she should tell the Brigadier. 'And sir?'

The Brigadier was just about to drive away. 'Yes?'

'I almost forgot. The Doctor told me to say that he'll be along soon.'

'How very kind of you to have remembered,' said the Brigadier. 'If it had crossed your mind to tell me earlier, I might have enjoyed the drive from London.' He let in the clutch, and the jeep drove away.

Jo went up to the door of the house and pulled an old-fashioned door bell. No bell rang inside; instead, the knob and some rusty wire came away in her hand. She put the knob down carefully on the step, and tapped on the door. Nothing happened. Cautiously she pushed the door, found it was unlocked. She looked inside.

'Hello?'

No answer. The walls of the hallway were whitewashed and clean but the hall had the musty smell of damp. Jo crept into the hall and followed a corridor leading to the back of the house. She found a door with a notice reading 'ROOM FOR LIVING', tapped, and looked into the room. It had a few old armchairs and a radio that might have come out of a museum. She went on down the corridor, found another door with a notice which read 'TOADSTOOLS, PROFESSORS, AND OTHER THINGS – WATCH IT!' Jo tapped on the door and was just about to push it open when a male voice bellowed, 'Come in!'

Jo went in. It was a sort of laboratory with a work bench, Bunsen burner, microscope and cupboards. A young man in blue jeans and a polo neck sweater was delicately taking a slice from a strange-looking fungus and mounting it on a microscope slide.

'Excuse me,' Jo started to say.

'Shut the blasted door,' shouted the young man, without looking up. 'It says outside "watch it", and you didn't.'

'Didn't what?'

'You didn't watch it.' He placed the slice of fungus on the slide and seemed satisfied. 'You could have ruined a month's work by letting the temperature in here drop half a degree.'

'How do you ever get in and out,' Jo asked, 'without opening the door sometimes?'

'Ah, good point,' said the young man. 'But I watch it. Understand?'

'No,' said Jo. 'But it doesn't matter. I'm Jo Grant, from London. I rang up and spoke to someone called Nancy, whoever she is. I've come to help Professor Jones.'

The young man flashed a glance at her. 'And how do you propose to help Professor Jones? You're not old enough.'

Jo was outraged but tried not show it. 'I've been assistant to an eminent scientist for some time, you know.'

'No, I didn't,' said the young man. 'How should I know if you don't tell me?'

'Well, I'm telling you!'

He stopped his work and looked at her, weighing her up. 'Know anything about entomology?'

'Insects? Yes, a little.'

'Then tell me,' said the young man, 'what's got twenty legs, a yellow body about two inches long and big red pincers on the front end?'

'I've no idea,' Jo answered.

'Pity,' said the young man, 'because there's one crawling up your left leg.'

Jo gave a screech, and brushed at her leg. But there was no insect. The young man had been joking.

'That wasn't very funny,' said Jo.

'It was from where I'm standing,' the man assured her. 'Why do you want to help this Professor Jones fellow?'

'I'd like to put a spanner in Panorama Chemicals' works.'

'I see,' said the man. 'Ever gone to bed hungry?'

'Not that I can remember. Why, is there nothing to eat in this house?'

The young man didn't answer the question, but continued with his own train of thought. 'Every night millions of people in the world go to sleep hungry. And those of us who do have enough food are starved of everything else a man needs to live like a man – '

Jo couldn't resist butting in. 'Do you always use the word "man" when you mean "human being"?'

The young man laughed. 'Oh, very good! After that, you'll never believe that I support women's liberation, will you? But please try to pardon a slip of the tongue.'

'Thank you,' said Jo. 'Now please continue.'

'Here at Wholeweal we're trying to find out how to live in a different way. We want to be human beings again – not slaves of machines and industry and finance.'

'Do you want a world without any machines at all?' asked Jo.

'That would be stupid,' said the young man. 'What matters is the type of machines we use.'

'What's your solution?'

'Solar energy,' he said emphatically. 'The sun is producing great quantities of energy, and we could use it. Instead, we burn oil one way and another, and pollute the air we breathe. And we could use the movement of the wind and the tides and the rivers. Are you warm enough?'

Jo was surprised at the question. 'Yes, thank you.'

'Heat from the river,' he explained. 'We have a waterwheel in the river at the back of the house. That drives an electrical generator and the electricity keeps the house warm. Alternative technology, you see. No waste. No pollution. Now Panorama Chemicals hope to produce 25% more petrol and diesel fuel from a given quantity of crude oil. But do you realise how they're going to do that?'

Jo shook her head. 'Not properly.'

'The process must be based on Bateson's polymerisation. And that means thousands of gallons of waste. A thick sludge you can't break down, like liquid plastic.' He paused. 'I think it's connected with the death of Ted Hughes.'

'The green man?' asked Jo. 'You mean they've been pumping this sludge down into the old mine here?'

He nodded. 'Could be.'

'That's terrible,' said Jo. She looked around the makeshift laboratory. 'What exactly are you doing in here?'

'Another side of our work,' said the young man. 'Very soon the world's going to need something to replace meat. A high protein fungus could be the answer.' He turned to her. 'Wholeweal isn't a place for drop-outs, you know.'

'I didn't imagine it was,' she said quickly.

'I agree that we've escaped from the rat race coming here,' he went on, 'the city pressures and the foul air. But we are trying to do things that may help the whole world.'

26

'This fungus idea,' said Jo, 'did Professor Jones think of that?'

'Professor Jones?' For a moment the young man seemed puzzled, then he smiled. 'Oh yes, one of his ideas. You've never met him I suppose?'

'Remember, I've only just arrived.'

'He can be pretty repulsive at times,' said the young man. 'Talks a lot about "love thy neighbour" then doesn't notice the people under his feet. He bites his fingernails and sometimes he just forgets to bath.'

'He is also a Nobel Prize winner,' said Jo, defensively, 'and a very brilliant man.'

'But he's only human – or do you regard him as a saint?'

Jo had read so much about the professor, she was affronted by this young man's remarks. 'Professor Clifford Jones is just about the most human human being alive today! And I think you're being very nasty about him.'

The door flew open. A plump woman, aged about thirty, came in and quickly closed the door behind her. 'Lunch is ready.' She noticed Jo. 'Oh, hello.'

'I'm Jo Grant,' said Jo.

'And I'm the girl you spoke to on the phone,' said the plump woman. She held out her hand. 'Nancy Banks, but everyone calls me Mum. I hope Cliff hasn't been talking too much nonsense to you.'

Jo turned in astonishment to the young man. 'Your name's Cliff?'

'At your service,' said the young man. 'Professor Clifford Jones.'

Jo's face filled with anger. 'And you let me go on saying those things?'

'They were very complimentary,' said Jones. 'It's nice to be the most human human being.'

While Jo was getting to know Professor Clifford Jones, a half mile away Brigadier Lethbridge Stewart was meeting Dr Thomas Stevens, director of Panorama Chemicals, in his modern air-conditioned office suite. Also present was Mark Elgin, the company's public relations officer.

'Security is the main consideration,' Dr Stevens was saying.

'Yes, of course,' agreed the Brigadier without thinking, because it seemed the right thing to say.

'There are these cranks down the road,' Dr Stevens went on, 'Professor Jones and his mob of idiots. Mind you, I recognise that the professor is a very clever young man. He won a Nobel Prize, you know?' He added this with some pride, as though it reflected on him personally to have such a celebrated enemy. 'We don't want him, or his kind, getting anything more about us in the newspapers.'

Mark Elgin spoke up, deferentially. 'The Minister of Energy has already imposed a D notice, sir.' D notices are sent to all newspapers, and to television and radio news services, when there is something the Government wants kept secret.

'That's come a bit late,' said Dr Stevens. 'Still, better late than never.'

'If I may ask,' said the Brigadier, 'had the death of the miner any connection with your company's activities?'

'I've absolutely no idea,' said Dr Stevens quickly.

Elgin changed the subject, to get away from the death. 'Brigadier, the Minister said you'd be bringing along some scientific chappie . . . ?'

'I hoped to,' said the Brigadier. 'He's on leave at the moment. If I may return to the question of the miner, I understand he had turned green . . .'

Neither Dr Stevens nor Mark Elgin said anything.

'Is that correct?' asked the Brigadier.

'My guess,' said Elgin, 'is that the poor man had a heart attack. He wasn't young, you know.'

'But why should he be green?' the Brigadier persisted.

'Look, Brigadier,' said Dr Stevens, 'your job here is to protect our establishment against hot-heads. Isn't that right?'

The Brigadier did not like being told what his job was. 'I feel it also my job, Dr Stevens, to find out about this man's death.'

'I see.' Dr Stevens stared out of his plate glass windows at the Welsh mountains in the distance. 'Then what do you propose to do?'

'If I may use your phone,' said the Brigadier, 'I'd like to see if my "scientific chappie" is back from leave yet.'

'By all means.' Dr Stevens pushed a slimline phone across the desk towards the Brigadier. 'But don't you know when your own people are supposed to report back for duty?'

The Brigadier started to dial UNIT Headquarters in London. 'Not with this particular man,' he said. 'He tends to take liberties with time.'

Two million light years away, the Doctor stood to catch his breath on a blue rock mountain. He was exhausted, having run to escape from the pecking blue birds and the blue unicorns.

'Wait till I tell the Time Lords about this,' he said to himself. 'It's the most unfriendly planet I've ever visited.'

Then he let out a cry as he felt something stick into his foot. Blue ants an inch long were swarming all over his left foot, digging through the shoe to get at the human flesh beneath. He brushed them off, and started climbing again.

Half an hour later he had reached the top of the little mountain. As far as the eye could see there were small

29

mountain peaks. In some of the valleys were lakes of deep blue water. They looked inviting, but the Doctor by now suspected them all to be filled with flesh-eating blue fish. He turned his attention to a cluster of sapphires embedded in the rock. As he reached out to take one, a shadow fell across him. Looking up he saw the huge talons of a blue eagle descending on him, its great wings flapping. The Doctor grabbed the sapphire, thrust it into his pocket, and ran for his life. The eagle flapped after him, its talons trying to grab at his head or shoulders. The Doctor zig-zagged, out-manoeuvring the big ungainly bird. He saw ahead a forest of blue trees, where the eagle could not follow, and made for it.

In the forest, safe from the eagle, the Doctor leant against a tree to recover his breath. Then he noticed that one of the lower branches of the tree was moving. As he turned to run again, the branch whipped round like a snake, but the Doctor was able to jump free. Still afraid of the eagle hovering outside the forest, he raced through the trees, avoiding the whiplash of living branches. Eventually he was through the forest, and back in the valley where the TARDIS had materialised.

He raced past beds of beautiful blue flowers that turned their gorgeous heads and spat stinging venom. Once more he heard the pounding of hooves, and turned to see at least a hundred blue unicorns charging towards him down a hill. From above came the flapping of the blue eagle's great wings – it had flown over the forest and was now swooping down with talons outstretched to tear at the Doctor's head. A violent streak of blue lightning suddenly raced across the sky, followed instantly by torrential blue rain.

All at once the ground beneath the Doctor's feet turned into wet blue slushy mud. Each step now was a great effort. However, the rain and mud did not slow down the blue unicorns. The leaders of the herd were racing against each other to be the first to drive their ugly twisted horns through the Doctor's body. Above, the eagle made more determined efforts to grab the Doctor, and a sharp talon split open his soaking wet jacket at the shoulder.

As the Doctor approached the TARDIS he saw squirming blue snakes writhing in the mud around the entrance. Hoping for the best, he took out his key, held it firmly in his hand, and charged straight at the door, aiming the key so that it would go into the lock without fumbling. The key slid in, he turned it, pushed the door open, and fell into the safety of the TARDIS, slamming the door behind him.

'So much for holidays on Metebelis Three,' he groaned, panting for breath, his clothes wringing wet. 'Next time I'll try Blackpool.'

A few moments later the TARDIS re-materialised in the Doctor's laboratory at UNIT Headquarters. The door opened and the Doctor tumbled out, his clothes still wet through. He sneezed violently. The telephone started to ring. He lifted the phone.

'Hello?'

'Ah, there you are, Doctor.' It was the Brigadier's voice. 'I'm speaking from Llanfairfach. Miss Grant told me that you might be coming down here after all. I'd like you to use the UNIT chopper and get here as quickly as possible.'

'Are there any unicorns there?' said the Doctor. He sneezed again.

The Brigadier laughed. 'I very much doubt it. Is that some little joke of yours, Doctor?'

'I'm not joking,' said the Doctor. 'What about eagles?'

'Not in Wales,' replied the Brigadier.

'What are the flowers like?'

There was a note of reprimand in the Brigadier's

voice. 'Doctor, the business at hand here is serious. But if you *must* know about the local flora, I did notice a few wild daffodils.'

'Good,' said the Doctor. 'Then I'll be there straight away!'

4

Into the Mine

The Brigadier replaced Dr Stevens's slimline telephone. 'Well, that's a start. The Doctor is on his way.'

'The Doctor?' asked Mark Elgin.

'My "scientific chappie", as you call him,' said the Brigadier.

'What was all that about daffodils?' asked Dr Stevens.

'The Doctor's a bit of a botanist,' said the Brigadier, lying quickly to cover his embarrassment. 'Now, gentlemen, if you'll excuse me, I think I'll take a look at that mine.'

'As I understand it, Brigadier,' said Dr Stevens, rising from his chair, 'your purpose here is to protect the interests of Panorama Chemicals?'

'And so it is,' agreed the Brigadier. 'There'll be no rabble breaking in to destroy your plant while UNIT's here. But I think it is also important for me to know more about that mine. So, if you'll excuse me . . . ' He smiled and made for the door.

'Of course,' said Dr Stevens. 'Mark, show the Brigadier out.'

Elgin opened the door. 'This way, sir.'

'Thank you.'

Dr Stevens watched them leave his office. Then he pressed a button on the inter-communication unit on his desk. 'Send in Hinks at once,' he said towards the built-in microphone.

33

While he waited for Hinks to arrive he stood at the window and looked out towards the mountains. Years ago he had enjoyed climbing mountains. But now his family had all deserted him, leaving a gap in his life that could only be filled by work. He was delighted when he was invited to become Director of the main British plant of Panorama Chemicals because he realised this was a job of such size and complexity he would be able to devote night and day to it. What he did not realise was that the job would provide him with the best and most faithful friend he had ever had.

His inter-com buzzed and the voice of his secretary, Stella, spoke through the built-in loudspeaker. 'I've located Mr Hinks, sir. He's on his way to your office.'

'Thank you,' Dr Stevens said to the inter-com.

He went back to studying the mountains. Maybe, he thought, he should try a little climbing again one day. Unfortunately he would not be able to take his new friend with him. But the exercise might do him good, and he loved the sense of history that emanated from those mountains.

Dr Stevens had enjoyed studying history when he was a boy at school. Sometimes he wished he was still there. But now he was a man and had the responsibilities of a man.

He turned from the window. His headache was starting to trouble him again. He wished Hinks would hurry and come to take orders, because he had to get rid of this headache.

There was a tap on the door and Hinks entered. 'You wanted me, sir?' Hinks was over six feet tall, and very broad-shouldered. He had a face like an ex-boxer who had lost too many fights.

The headache was very bad now. 'I want you to . . .' Dr Stevens knew he was swaying slightly with the pain. 'I want you to . . .'

'Are you all right, sir?' Although Hinks asked the

34

question politely there was ice in his voice. There always was.

'The mine,' said Dr Stevens, 'nobody must go down the mine.'

'I'll see to it,' said Hinks, grinning. The prospect of any kind of violence always made Hinks grin. 'Sure you're all right, sir?'

'Perfectly all right,' Dr Stevens lied. 'Just see no one goes down the mine. That'll be all.'

'Right you are, sir.' Hinks turned and went. Dr Stevens hated to imagine what Hinks might do to stop people going down the mine.

Alone, Dr Stevens staggered over to the door and locked it. Then he crossed back to his desk, unlocked a little cupboard built into the side of the desk. His hands were now shaking, and his head felt like splitting open. He reached into the cupboard and brought out a very special pair of earphones. Fumbling, he put them on, plugged the lead into a special socket in his desk intercom, and slumped back into his chair. The voice of his friend Boss at once started to talk to him through the earphones, reassuring Dr Stevens that what he was doing was right. Almost immediately the headache went away.

Jo was pleased with the way Nancy, or Mum, had welcomed her, but she was still angry with Professor Clifford Jones. Over lunch she met a number of the Wholeweal Community, mainly young people who had come to Llanfairfach because they were fed up with the pressures and materialism and pollution of the big cities. Conversation during the meal was light hearted, and they seemed pleased to have this newcomer, Jo, in their midst. But as soon as the meal was over they all went back to their various occupations. The Nut Hatch was a hive of activity, where these young people spent their time evolving alternative methods of production and living. Jo

Boss started to talk to him through the earphones

helped Nancy wash up the dishes. Then she had nothing
to do. Everyone was far too busy to involve her, or even
talk to her. Burning with curiosity about the man who
died and went green, she decided to go and look at the
mine.

The closed mine looked sadly derelict. Grass and
weeds grew over the little narrow gauge railway lines
once used for pushing wheeled tubs of coal. Immediately
over the shaft was a high metal construction with wheels
at the top. This was part of the lift mechanism. When
a coal mine is in full life, the wheels at the top of these
metal constructions are turning all the time, either taking
miners down to work, or bringing up the coal they have
hewn from the bowels of the earth – but here everything
was ghostly still.

As Jo wandered about among mounds of coal dust,
the unused wheeled tubs, and the outhouses and sheds
around the main shaft, a man came out of the pit office
and shouted at her.

'Hey!' he called. 'What are you doing?'

Jo went over to him. Like many Welshmen he was
short and dark eyed.

'I'm from UNIT,' she said. 'I want to look at the mine.'

'Well now you've seen it,' said the man. 'So go away.
You can't walk round here without authority.'

'Where do I get it?'

'National Coal Board,' said the man, 'in Cardiff.'

'You're just trying to be awkward,' said Jo.

As he spoke, another short dark-eyed man popped his
head out from the office and called something urgently
in Welsh. The man talking to Jo turned and rushed into
the office. Jo followed and stood at the door. The office
was small and untidy, its wooden floor black with in-
grained coal dust. A door led off to the lift machinery.
The man who talked to Jo had grabbed an old-fashioned
telephone. He listened, then spoke in rapid Welsh.

'What's happening?' Jo asked quietly.

The second man said, 'One of our mates, Dai Evans, has gone down the pit. Now he's in trouble.' He was too worried to ask who Jo was or to tell her to go away.

With one man on the phone, and Jo and the other man watching him, none of them saw or heard Hinks as he quietly slipped into the lift machinery by way of its outer door. Hinks was no engineer, but the lift machinery was simple enough for him to understand. In a couple of seconds he was able to sabotage the machinery and make his getaway.

The man put down the phone. 'We've got to get him out – quickly!' He noticed Jo standing by the door. 'I told you, girl, go away!'

'If someone's hurt,' she said, 'I could be useful. I'm trained in first aid.'

'Women don't go down the pit,' said the second man.

'Those poor little pit ponies you used to have years ago down in the mines,' said Jo, 'did they all have to be males?'

'There's a daft question for you,' said the second man.

'If female ponies can go down a mine,' said Jo, 'so can female humans. Especially if they can be useful. I'm Jo Grant. Who are you two?'

'Dave Griffiths,' said the first man.

'Bert Williams,' said the second.

'Which of you is coming with me?' asked Jo.

'There's cheek for you!' said Bert Williams. 'Who said you were going?'

'Could either of you put a splint on a broken leg?' asked Jo. 'Or know how to give the kiss of life?'

Neither answered.

'So you see,' said Jo. 'You need me. How do we get down there?'

'I'll take her with me,' said Bert. 'Perhaps she could be useful.' He turned to Jo. 'We must get a helmet to fit you, miss, although with a head as big as yours that might be difficult. Come along.'

Bert led Jo across to one of the locker rooms, a long low building with rows of metal lockers where the miners used to leave their working clothes. There were helmets on the shelves, and Bert found one to fit Jo. On the front of the helmet was fastened an electric lamp. Thus equipped, they went back to the pit head office.

'Has he phoned again?' Bert asked.

'Nothing,' said Dave.

'All right,' said Bert, 'get ready to operate the machinery.'

Dave hurried into the room containing the lift machinery. Bert put on his helmet, and took Jo away from the office towards the lift. It was like a cage, large enough to carry twenty men at a time.

'This isn't like a lift you'll find in a shop,' said Bert. 'We don't go down slowly and gradually, with someone to tell you what you can buy on the different floors. Once we start moving, we drop like a ruddy stone, and you can see everything go by.'

'I'm not frightened,' Jo fibbed.

'I was the first time,' said Bert. 'Fourteen years old I was, and scared out of my wits, but I tried not to show it.'

The cage started to move.

'Here we go,' said Bert. 'Hold tight.'

Suddenly the floor of the cage dropped away from under Jo's feet. She felt very sick.

As the big wheels above the lift shaft began to spin, they were observed by the Brigadier and the Doctor. They had just arrived in the Brigadier's jeep.

'I thought this mine was closed,' said the Doctor.

'It is, or supposed to be.' The Brigadier stopped the jeep and ran to the pit head machine room, the Doctor close behind. They found Dave Griffiths at the controls. 'Who's going down the mine?' asked the Brigadier.

'One of my mates and some girl or other,' said Dave. 'What's it to you?'

'A girl?' said the Doctor. 'Please stop the lift immediately.'

'There's a mate of mine hurt down there,' said Dave. 'In some kind of trouble.'

'All the more reason to stop winding!' shouted the Doctor. The look on his face was imploring, the tone of voice imperative.

'Right you are,' said Dave. He pulled on the brake. Nothing happened. He pulled harder. The wheels of the lift mechanism kept spinning. 'I *can't* stop it,' he screamed, 'it's out of control. Clutch and brake both gone.'

The Doctor noticed an old iron bar lying on the blackened floor. He picked it up and wedged it against the main drum of the machinery. 'Now reverse the motor,' he called.

'It won't work,' said Dave. 'We'll snap the cable.'

'Don't argue, man,' said the Doctor. 'It's their only chance.' As he spoke he braced himself and pulled harder on the wedged iron bar.

Dave put the electrical motor into reverse. There was a shower of sparks and smoke bellowed out from the machinery. Then it stopped. The Doctor released his grip on the iron rod. 'That's done it,' he said.

'That,' said Dave, 'has seized up the whole works.'

The Brigadier looked at a meter on the wall that showed the depth of either of the twin lifts. 'According to this, you halted their descent just twenty feet before they hit the bottom. Congratulations.'

'It's all right you congratulating us,' said Dave, 'but I told you, the machine's seized solid now. Wherever they are in that lift shaft, they've got to hang there until we solve this problem.'

Jo and Bert picked themselves up from the floor of the

40

cage. The force of the sudden stopping had thrown them both down.

'You all right?' Bert asked.

'No bones broken,' replied Jo. 'Why have we stopped here?'

'Maybe I should write a letter to the National Coal Board and ask them,' said Bert. 'Seriously, I think it was a brake failure. Can't happen in theory.'

'I've heard those theories before,' said Jo. 'How do we get out of here?'

'First let's find out how high we are,' said Bert. He took a screwdriver from his pocket, and dropped it over the side of the cage into the total darkness below, and listened as it hit the ground beneath. 'I reckon we're about twenty feet from the bottom.'

'A good thing we stopped,' remarked Jo.

'Yes. Another two or three seconds and we'd have had our thigh bones up under our arm pits.' He looked around the cage. 'I think we may be in luck,' he said, finding a rope in a coil attached to the wall of the cage. 'Ever shinned down a rope before, miss?'

'More than once,' said Jo. 'How do we know it's long enough?'

Bert was paying out the rope, measuring it with the span of his arms. 'There's a good twenty feet here.'

'You only *guessed* we're twenty feet from the bottom,' Jo reminded him.

'Good point,' said Bert. 'It's a logical young woman you are. So I'll go first. If I run out of rope and drop ten feet, you may get a chance to fix a couple of those splints you were talking about to two broken legs.' He attached the rope to the frame of the cage, paid it out over the side, then climbed after it. 'Don't forget we're down here to help a man in trouble, so maybe we should take a risk or two.'

The Doctor completed his inspection of the lift machinery. He wiped his hands on a brightly coloured handkerchief drawn from one of his capacious jacket pockets, and spoke to Dave and the Brigadier.

'Absolutely correct diagnosis of the situation,' he said. 'It's seized solid. Wherever that lift is hanging in the shaft, it's going to be there for quite some time.'

'I noticed coming here,' said the Brigadier, 'there are two shafts. Couldn't we use the other lift?'

Dave shook his head at the simplicity of this English non-miner. 'It's a counterweight lift system, man. As one goes down the other comes up. So if one is jammed, the other is jammed, too.'

'That makes sense,' said the Doctor, 'although it doesn't help very much.' He scratched the side of his nose and considered the problem. 'What if we made that other lift independent?'

'By Jove,' said the Brigadier. 'You mean so that it could work on its own?'

'That,' said the Doctor, 'is what "independent" means.' He turned back to Dave. 'Couldn't we rig a donkey engine and pulley system?'

'I suppose we could,' said Dave. 'But remember it's the same cable running to both lifts. 'We'd have to cut through that cable to free the other lift before we could do anything.'

'All right,' said the Doctor. 'Where's your cutting gear?'

'There isn't any,' said Dave. 'The mine's been out of action for a year. When it closed, the National Coal Board stripped it of everything.'

'Then for goodness' sake,' said the Doctor, showing a touch of anger, 'let's tell the National Coal Board we need back the cutting gear, and we need it fast!'

'Have you ever tried to get the Board to do *anything* fast?' asked Dave. 'But I've been thinking. I know where there should be the equipment we need.'

'Where?'

'Panorama Chemicals,' said Dave, 'if they're willing to help us.'

The Brigadier moved to go. 'I'll get over there and ask them straight away!'

'Hold your horses, man,' said Dave. 'We're not all savages in Wales, you know. We've got telephones, just like you English. Come along with me.'

Dave led the Doctor and the Brigadier back into the pit head office. He looked up the number he wanted in a grubby school exercise book, then picked up the phone and dialled.

Dr Arnold Bell placed his carefully prepared report on the big desk in Dr Stevens's office. He had expected Dr Stevens to be there, but found the office deserted. As Chief Scientific Officer of Panorama Chemicals he felt free to wander into the Director's office, especially when he had such an important report as this to deliver. The report stated in analytical detail that Bateson's polymerisation method was definitely working. It meant that for every ton of crude oil imported from the Middle East, or mined in the North Sea, Panorama Chemicals would be able to produce 25% more petrol or diesel fuel. The additional profit of the company might run into millions and millions of pounds. However, Dr Bell was not concerned with profits – that was Dr Stevens's affair. What fascinated Dr Bell was the scientific achievement. The method resulted in tons of waste fluid, and this would have to be deposited somewhere. But Dr Bell did not regard that as his problem. For the time being the waste was being pumped into the old coal mine. No doubt in time the company would devise some other means of disposal.

As he turned to leave the office the desk phone rang. He picked up the receiver.

'Bell speaking.'

'Is that Panorama Chemicals?' The voice had a strong Welsh accent.

'Yes,' said Dr Bell, 'you've come through on a direct line to the Director's office. Can I help you?'

'I'm calling from the mine,' the voice went on. 'One of the lifts has jammed. There are people trapped. We need cable-cutting equipment. Can you help us?'

'Is anyone hurt?' Dr Bell was genuinely concerned.

'We don't know that yet,' said the voice. 'Maybe they are only suspended near the bottom of the shaft. We need cutting equipment to free the other lift and work it independently if we can.'

'I'm sure we can help –'

As Dr Bell spoke the office door opened and Dr Stevens walked in followed by Hinks. Dr Bell told the caller to hang on, then quickly relayed the message to Dr Stevens. He expected Dr Stevens to give immediate orders for the company's cutting equipment to be rushed to the mine. Instead, Dr Stevens crossed to his desk and disconnected the phone.

'It is not company policy to lend equipment,' said Dr Stevens. There seemed to be something strange about his voice.

Dr Bell, the now dead telephone still in his hand, could not believe his ears. 'But people are trapped. It could be a matter of life and death!'

'I'm sorry, Dr Bell, but as from this moment we have no cutting equipment.'

'That is ridiculous,' said Dr Bell. 'I know where it is!'

'And there it shall remain.' Dr Stevens seated himself behind his large desk. 'What's more, it may be necessary for you to confirm to other people that we have no cutting equipment.'

Dr Bell began to realise that the Director was being perfectly serious. 'Would you mind explaining to me why on earth we shouldn't help these people?'

44

'The mine must not be investigated,' said Dr Stevens. 'You know that as well as I do.'

'Because that miner died?'

'That, and other reasons.' Dr Stevens noticed the report lying on his desk, smiled and changed the subject. 'Ah, that looks interesting . . . ' He opened the cover.

'One death is enough,' said Dr Bell. 'I'm going to get that equipment to them.' He turned to leave and found Hinks had placed himself in front of the door. 'Will you get out of my way, please?'

'Stay where you are, Hinks,' said Dr Stevens. 'He must not leave.'

Dr Bell swung round. 'Look here, you have no right to keep me prisoner –'

But his outburst was interrupted by a booming voice that seemed to come from the ceiling.

'Stevens?'

Dr Stevens looked up, 'Yes?'

'Process him.'

'Is that wise?' asked Dr Stevens, speaking to the ceiling.

'It is necessary,' said the booming voice. 'Do as I say. Process.'

'Who on earth was that?' asked Dr Bell, mystified by the brief exchange.

'Our boss,' said Dr Stevens. 'Yours and mine.'

'I . . . I don't understand.'

'You will,' said Dr Stevens. 'Very soon.'

Jo lowered herself slowly down the rope. As she swung to and fro the beam from her helmet played like a search-light as it swept the sides of the lift shaft. Looking down she could see the light from Bert's helmet as he looked up towards her.

'You've got another three feet of rope,' he called. 'Then

45

you'll have to fall the rest of the way. I'm here to catch you.'

She continued to ease herself down the rope. Then, as she expected, she felt no more rope between her legs. She lowered herself another couple of feet and let go, bringing up her knees a little to make her legs more springy for the final impact. For a moment she fell through space, then hit the ground. Bert caught her to steady her.

'Where is he?'

'Over here.'

Bert led the way to where Dai Evans lay moaning on the floor of the mine.

'Look,' said Bert. 'Look at his arm.'

Jo looked down, her helmet light playing on Dai Evans.

His hand and arm were glowing a bright green.

5

Escape!

The Brigadier's jeep screeched to a halt outside the Panorama Chemicals building. He leapt out, ran up the steps. A uniformed attendant rushed to hold open one of the glass doors.

'I need to see Dr Stevens,' said the Brigadier. 'A matter of the utmost importance.'

The urgency in his voice impressed the attendant, and he hurriedly escorted the Brigadier to the Director's office and tapped on the door.

Dr Stevens was sitting at his desk, in conference with Mark Elgin. They broke off their discussion and listened attentively while the Brigadier explained what had just happened at the mine and the pressing need for cable-cutting equipment. The Brigadier also mentioned that Dr Stevens's phone seemed to be out of order. Apparently Dave Griffiths made contact when he dialled, but then the line went suddenly dead.

'First things first,' said Dr Stevens when the Brigadier had finished. 'Thanks for letting us know about the phone. However, the immediate problem is the equipment you need, and we shall be glad to help you in any way possible.' He touched a button on his desk inter-com and spoke towards the microphone. 'Dr Bell, could you come in here a moment, please?'

'At once,' said Dr Bell's voice over the tiny loudspeaker.

'Dr Bell is our scientific and technical officer,' Dr

47

Stevens explained. 'Very meticulous worker, an idealist in his way. Many's the time I've had to tell him not to work all night – to go home to his wife and children.'

'How excellent,' said the Brigadier, although he wasn't at all interested. His mind was fixed on the people who were trapped in the mine. 'Will he take long to get here?'

'Hardly,' Mark Elgin smiled. 'He works just down the corridor.'

There was a tap on the door and a spare ascetic man in a white coat entered. 'You wanted me, Dr Stevens?'

'Our good friend the Brigadier needs our help,' said Dr Stevens. 'Apparently there's been another accident in the mine.'

The Brigadier swung round to greet Dr Bell. 'Good afternoon, Doctor. We desperately need cutting equipment – oxyacetylene, that sort of thing, and we need it fast.'

Dr Bell shook his head. 'I'm sorry, Brigadier, but we have nothing of that kind here.'

The Brigadier was astounded. 'In an industrial undertaking of this size?'

Dr Stevens also seemed most surprised. 'But surely, Dr Bell, we should have all sorts of emergency equipment? What's happened to it?'

Dr Bell shrugged. 'The emergency equipment was withdrawn some time ago, sir, to be replaced by thermic lances. They haven't arrived yet.'

'But that's incredible,' said Elgin. 'I'm no technician, but I'm sure I saw oxyacetylene equipment in the stores only last week.'

Dr Stevens gave him a hard piercing look. 'As you said, you are no technician. I'm sure Dr Bell knows what he is talking about.' He turned to the Brigadier and smiled. 'You must think we are woefully ill-equipped.'

'I do find it rather surprising,' the Brigadier commented.

48

Dr Stevens rose from his desk. 'I hope you won't accuse us of being deliberately obstructive, Brigadier.' He took the Brigadier's arm and started to propel him out of the office in a friendly way. 'Have you thought of asking Professor Jones? Ah but no, I remember. They tried to borrow our equipment some weeks ago, so presumably they don't have any themselves.'

Dr Stevens led the Brigadier away, still talking. Elgin found himself staring at Dr Bell.

'I can't believe this,' said Elgin. 'We must have some sort of cutting tools here.'

'I had given an exact account of the position,' said Dr Bell. He spoke as though he had rehearsed the sentence.

Elgin looked closely at Dr Bell. 'Are you feeling all right?'

'I feel perfectly well, thank you.'

'But your voice,' Elgin persisted. 'It doesn't sound like *you*.'

'I must get on with my work,' said Dr Bell. He moved towards the door.

'No, hang on a moment. I think it's time we had a chat about our revered Director, Dr Stevens.'

Dr Bell paused by the door. 'What about Dr Stevens?'

Elgin had always liked Dr Bell and felt he could speak his mind to him. 'It strikes me as odd how he wants to hush up the death of the miner who turned green. Is there something going on that no one's told me?'

'I cannot discuss our Director with you, Elgin.'

'Elgin?' Elgin went up close and looked Dr Bell in the eyes. 'You always call me Mark. What's the matter with you?'

Dr Bell put his hand on the door handle, ready to go. 'Your attitude will be reported. Disloyalty cannot be tolerated.'

'Disloyalty?' said Elgin. 'You're talking like a robot!'

'The Director will hear of this,' said Dr Bell. He turned

the handle, opened the door, and marched off down the corridor.

Elgin watched as Dr Bell went away. Even his walk seemed different. Elgin suddenly shivered. He felt most uneasy.

'Are you scared?' Bert's voice was gentle.

'I am a bit,' said Jo. 'What's that creaking sound?'

Bert listened. From the depths of the mine came a slight creaking noise. 'That's nothing,' he said. 'We say the old girl – the mine, that is – is snoring in her sleep. It's the roof moving a bit.'

Jo felt her knees shaking. 'It's going to fall in?'

'Shall we say it's *trying* to.' He grinned. 'That's what all the props are for.'

'Have you ever been trapped?' she asked.

He nodded, the beam of his helmet light playing up and down the mine wall as he moved his head. 'Eight years ago next November. I'd just finished my snap – lunch, as you would call it. Then a section of the roof came down. We didn't see daylight again for the next two days.'

'But you were all safe?'

This time he shook his head, his helmet light playing horizontally to and fro across the mine wall. 'Six of us never saw daylight again.'

Jo was shocked. 'That's terrible.'

He shrugged. 'You know how many miners are killed a year in the pits? Fifty, on average. Makes you think, doesn't it? Anyway, I shouldn't be telling you these terrible things when we're stuck down here!' He walked over and looked at Dai Evans. Dai had stopped moaning. His face was turning bright green.

'Do you think they're doing anything to get us out?' Jo asked.

'Must be by now,' said Bert. 'But I've been thinking.

50

Maybe it's time we started to get ourselves out.'

'How?'

'That fall eight years ago,' he said, trying to remember. 'They finally got us out through an old shaft. Of course, it may have fallen in by now – it wasn't in regular use. I don't want to lead you on a wild goose chase if I can't find it again ... '

'Anything's better than sitting here waiting,' said Jo, getting to her feet.

'That's where you're wrong. Getting lost in one of the galleries could be a lot worse than sitting on our backsides hoping for help from up top. But if I could remember the way we went . . . ' He haunched down, and started to draw a map of the mine in the coal dust on the floor.

'We'd take Dai Evans with us, of course?' Jo asked tentatively.

Bert looked up at her. 'He'd hold us back, miss. In any case, the way he looks, I don't think he'll be seeing daylight again. Ever.'

In the pit head office Dave Griffiths dialled the phone number of the National Coal Board offices in Cardiff. Watching him was Professor Jones, who with a few other local people had come running to the mine on hearing of yet another accident. A girl answered the phone.

'This is Llanfairfach here,' said Dave into the phone. 'Let me speak to Mr Ron Owen, if you please.'

'I'll try to find him for you,' said the girl and went off the line.

'Surely,' queried Professor Jones, 'there must be another way down into the mine?'

'Uneconomic to have more than one shaft,' said Dave, waiting for Mr Owen to come to the telephone. 'The old private owners were in coal for profit, weren't they?' He heard Mr Owen speaking on the phone. 'That you, Ron?

51

Dave Griffiths here. There's been another accident – '

The Doctor stepped through the door from the room containing the lift machinery. 'That's where you're wrong,' he cut in.

Dave asked Mr Owen to hold on for a moment. 'What are you talking about, Doctor?'

'I'm saying that what happened was not an accident,' the Doctor repeated. He put a metal cotter pin on the desk for Dave to see. 'That was lying on the floor near the cages. It had been removed from the brake linkage. What's happened to the lifts was deliberate sabotage!'

'You could be right,' said Dave. 'Anyway, we still need cutting equipment.' He turned to the phone to report the latest incident at Llanfairfach colliery.

As he did so, the Brigadier returned from Panorama Chemicals. He threw his swagger cane down onto the desk, next to the cotter pin. 'Can you believe it, Doctor? A place the size of that chemical works, and no cutting gear!' Then he noticed the cotter pin. 'What's that?'

The Doctor explained his discovery. There was no way the cotter pin could have fallen out of the brake linkage. It had been pulled out by someone who wanted to create an 'accident'.

'You say Panorama have no cutting gear?' asked the young Professor Jones, puzzled by this news.

'I saw both the Director there and their chief scientific and technical officer,' said the Brigadier. 'May I ask who you are, sir?'

Professor Jones didn't bother to answer the question. He turned to Dave Griffiths, who had just put down the phone. 'Dave, didn't you borrow cutting equipment from Panorama only a fortnight ago?'

Dave nodded. 'They let me collect it and put it back myself. It's in the storage shed at the back of the power house there.'

Professor Jones turned back to the Brigadier. 'You should have insisted.'

'Should I?' said the Brigadier, who did not take kindly to being told what to do by a stranger. 'If I may repeat my question, are you connected with this mine in some way?'

'This is Professor Jones,' said Dave, with a touch of pride. 'He's come to live in the village.'

'Professor Jones?' said the Doctor, beaming and extending his hand. 'I never realised. I've been wanting to meet you for a long time. Your paper on DNA synthesis was quite remarkable for your age.'

Professor Jones took the Doctor's remark as a slight rebuff for his being so young. 'You regard me as, shall we say, a "promising youngster"? – not to be taken too seriously?'

'No, no,' said the Doctor. 'I mean for the age you live in. I haven't seen anything like that paper of yours since a fellow I met in Vladivostok in the year 2179.'

Professor Jones and Dave Griffiths stared at the Doctor. 'The year 2179?' said Professor Jones. 'You mean 205 years in the future?' A smile played on the young professor's lips. Clearly he thought the Doctor was mad.

'Well, maybe it was the year 2169. Anyway, it doesn't really matter. You're a very remarkable young scientist, and it's an honour to meet you.'

The Brigadier cleared his throat, loudly. 'Doctor, the matter at hand is the rescue of Miss Grant and the man she went with down the mine.'

Professor Jones said, 'Why don't we go back to Panorama Chemicals and just *take* the equipment we need, by force if necessary?'

'Hold on,' said the Brigadier. 'I can't start a war with Panorama Chemicals! I'm supposed to be protecting them from demonstrators and possible sabotage! In fact, Professor Jones, I am supposed to be protecting them against you. Now, to be practical, where's the nearest town where we could hire this stuff?'

53

Dave said, 'Newport, I imagine. But it's quite a drive.'

'Then I had better get started,' said the Brigadier. 'Exactly where in Newport?'

'There's a company I know of hire out all sorts of tools and equipment,' said Dave. 'What if I come with you? Might save time.'

'I should be most grateful,' the Brigadier accepted. 'Doctor, we'll be back as quickly as possible. I trust you will not involve yourself in anything between now and then that might possibly upset the status quo.'

The Brigadier hurried out, followed by Dave Griffiths. A moment later the Doctor heard the jeep start up and tear away at high speed.

'That army friend of yours,' said Professor Jones. 'He seems to be a great believer in law and order.'

'Aren't we all?' asked the Doctor. 'At least, when there *is* law and order to believe in.' He picked up the cotter pin again and looked at it thoughtfully. 'Who would have done a criminal thing like this?'

'Certainly not one of the miners,' said Professor Jones.

'Exactly,' said the Doctor. 'Nor any of the other villagers because they are all related to miners.' He looked up and smiled at the younger man. 'People from the Wholeweal Community, perhaps?' It was more of a joke than a serious question. 'So, who else? And why?' He scratched his chin. 'You know, Panorama Chemicals is beginning to interest me. Do you know the layout there?'

'Very well,' said Professor Jones. 'Are you thinking what I'm thinking, Doctor?'

Hinks was sitting back in his own little room in the security sector of the Panorama Chemicals building. There was nothing much to do, so he had made himself a cup of tea and was now reading one of his comics. He had a big collection of comics, mainly American, most of them full of pictures that told stories. He preferred

54

pictures to words because he could not read very fast, although he tried to keep this a secret. Hinks had looked through the picture story many times before, but it always fascinated him to go through it again. He was just about to turn the page that carried the first picture of the torture sequence when an alarm buzzer in his room started to bleep. Angrily he put down the comic, picked up a phone.

'What is it?'

'Demonstrators,' replied the voice of a security guard. 'Lots of them.'

Hinks switched on the television monitor screen by his bed. It immediately showed the view around the front gates. Professor Clifford Jones and a crowd of young people from the Wholeweal Community were parading up and down in the road, banging drums, playing musical instruments, and shouting slogans. He turned up the volume to hear what they were shouting.

'Save the valleys from Panorama Chemicals . . . PC stands for pollution and corruption . . . Stevens must go – the further the better.'

Hinks snapped off the sound, picked up the phone again. He barked orders into the mouthpiece. 'All security units to the front section. Under no circumstances must they be allowed to break into the grounds.'

Regretfully he put away his comic, got up to go and protect the building. Still, the comic would be there when he got back. And he hadn't yet got to the pictures of people being beaten and burned, so he had something to look foward to.

From his position high in a tree, the Doctor could just see the noisy demonstration taking place at the front gates of Panorama Chemicals. He waited until he saw security guards run to take up their positions against the possibility of the demonstrators trying to break in. Then, with great

55

care, he crawled along the one branch of the tree that had grown over the electrified fence which surrounded the building. As he neared the end of the branch it began to sag under his weight, almost touching the fence below. The Doctor knew that if it did make contact, a charge of electricity would course through the branch, and through him, too, and that it was probably powerful enough to kill. With the tree branch barely an inch from the fence, the Doctor gave a final little jump – and landed on his feet inside the compound. He released his hold on the branch a fraction of a second before it came into contact with the fence. There was a flash, and it withered and fell from the tree.

The Doctor paused a moment to consult the map which Professor Jones had sketched for him. Then he raced across open ground towards the buildings.

From his office Dr Stevens looked down at the demonstrators. He had hoped UNIT was going to stop all this nonsense. In his mind he started to formulate a strong letter of protest to the Government, complaining that Brigadier Lethbridge Stewart seemed more involved in the colliery than in protecting Panorama Chemicals. These idiots, Dr Stevens thought, banging drums and shouting, might have good intentions, but they were not realists. What the world wanted was more and more petrol and diesel, for industry, areoplanes, and road vehicles. As for pollution caused through the continued use of oil, that was the price mankind had to pay. But in time, Dr Stevens believed, even this problem could be solved. Professor Jones and his followers lived in a world of make-believe. The clock of technological progress could not be turned back.

As he watched from his window he saw Hinks run out to give orders to the security guards. Dr Stevens did not like Hinks. He seemed to be a survival from an

earlier brutish age, a very violent sort of man. But, Dr
Stevens reminded himself, the price he paid to keep
Panorama Chemicals secure from hot-heads like Professor
Jones was to employ thugs like Hinks. It saddened the
idealistic side of Dr Stevens's thinking that nothing was
for nothing.

His thoughts were interrupted by a ring on the internal
phone. He lifted it.

'Yes?'

'A stranger is in the grounds,' said a guard's voice.
'He appears to be consulting a map of the grounds, and is
making for the equipment sheds. Should we destroy him?'

Dr Stevens immediately realised the trick. All the
shouting and drum banging at the front gates was a
decoy. 'No,' he said into the phone. 'Catch him, then
tell me where to find him.'

He put down the phone. Was this anything to do with
the Brigadier's request for cutting gear? If so, he had a
surprise up his sleeve.

The Doctor paused by the side of a building and looked
at the sketch map again. He was, he calculated, now
quite close to the equipment shed. Committing the route
to memory he put the map into his pocket and strode
along the side of the building. He knew he should shortly
turn right and pass through a narrow passageway that
ran between two buildings.

He turned the corner and saw the passageway. The
equipment sheds, according to the map, were at the far
end. From the distance he could hear the demonstrators
shouting and singing. Smiling to himself he set off down
the passageway. As he reached the middle a metal grille
slammed across the way ahead of him. He wheeled round.
Another metal grille closed behind him. He looked up
to see if there was anywhere to climb. The face of Hinks
grinned down at him from a low roof.

The grinning face of Hinks looked down at him

'This is your friendly host,' called Hinks. 'We hope your stay at Panorama will be long and uncomfortable.' He guffawed loudly. It was not often Hinks had the opportunity to make a joke.

Jo and Bert paused in their trudge along the mine.

'Do you really think you're going to find this old shaft?' she asked.

Bert wiped the sweat from his brow. 'I don't know. Let's take a breather.'

They both sank down, sitting on the floor with their backs to the wall.

'Did you ever think of becoming anything else?' Jo asked.

'Than a miner?' Bert gave a short laugh. 'Oh yes, I thought about becoming a film star, or winning the football pools. Every man thinks about it, but not many actually *do* it.'

'But it seems so dangerous,' Jo said. 'And such a terrible place to work.'

'Think we're simple-minded, do you?' There was a gentle smile in his voice as he put the question.

'I wouldn't say that,' she answered. 'But . . . well, why do people become miners?'

'You don't get much choice,' he said simply. 'There's some people get born in Buckingham Palace, and they becomes kings and queens, because that's the family occupation. Us, we get born in a place like Llanfairfach, where our fathers and uncles all go down the pit. When you're old enough you go down too, to show the world you're a man. Daft, isn't it?'

'Not really,' she said. 'Someone has to get the coal.'

'That's true.' He was quiet for a moment. 'There's more to it than that, miss. When you're a miner you are part of one big family, and that's a wonderful feeling. Every man in the pits knows his life depends on the other men. We live together, we die together, and' – he grinned broadly – 'by goodness if the people up top don't treat us right, we go on strike together!'

'It's really like being a member of another nation,' she said.

Bert got to his feet. 'That's exactly how it is, miss. There's us down here, and there's them up there.' He stopped, and looked back the way they had come. 'And there's poor Dai where we left him, probably dead by now.' He turned back to Jo. 'Well, let's see if we can find our way out of here, is it?'

Jo got up, and they continued to trudge down the long black gallery of the mine.

'Who are you?'

Dr Stevens, flanked by Hinks and security guards, stared at the Doctor through the metal grille. Some little distance away Mark Elgin stood watching.

'Most people call me the Doctor. And may I ask who you are, sir?'

'My name is Stevens – Dr Stevens. I am the Director of this project.'

'Delighted to meet you.' The Doctor was about to put his hand through the grille to shake hands with his captor, when he realised it might be electrified. He withdrew quickly.

'Now that you know who I am,' continued Dr Stevens, 'perhaps you would care to elaborate about yourself?'

'I am attached to UNIT as a scientific adviser,' said the Doctor. 'Does that clarify the situation?'

Dr Stevens smiled. 'Of course, the errant Doctor. We've been hoping you'd arrive, although not quite like this. Do you normally break into private property, especially when you'd be more than welcome arriving at the front door?'

'I do very little *normally*,' said the Doctor, 'unless that is the quickest way to go about things. In this instance, an abnormal approach seemed more fitting. We urgently need cable-cutting equipment at the mine. You refused to give it. Yet my information is that it is stored in that shed over there.'

'May I ask where you got this information?' said Dr Stevens.

'From someone to whom you loaned the equipment only recently,' replied the Doctor.

'Well,' said Dr Stevens, 'we certainly *did* have that kind of equipment here. But not now. It's all been returned to our main stores in another part of the country. But to put your mind at rest, let us investigate.'

He pressed a button on the wall and the metal grille slid out of the way. Without a word Dr Stevens, accompanied by Hinks, crossed a concrete area to the equipment shed. Dr Stevens nodded and Hinks produced a key and unlocked the doors. The shed was completely empty.

'You see?' said Dr Stevens.

'It seems I've been misinformed,' said the Doctor.

'Believe me, Doctor,' said Dr Stevens, as he now walked the Doctor away from the empty shed, 'Panorama Chemicals always tries to be a good neighbour. Our plant in Ethiopia has distributed thousands of tons of grain to the starving. In Persia and Saudi Arabia all local employees have free classes to learn to read and write their own languages.'

'Most impressive,' said the Doctor politely, even though he was being gently escorted off the premises.

'If we had anything that could help the people of Llanfairfach,' Dr Stevens went on, 'we'd be only too glad to give it.'

From where Mark Elgin stood he could hear Dr Stevens's voice fading away as he, the Doctor and Hinks went out of sight. Elgin crossed to the now open equipment shed and looked inside. He had passed this

61

way only yesterday and had caught sight of masses of equipment in the shed. Where had it all gone? And why?

The Brigadier felt pleased with himself. Halfway to Newport he and Dave Griffiths had passed through a small town with an extraordinarily long Welsh name where the Brigadier had spotted the words 'Crash Repairs' over a local garage. He stopped the jeep immediately and called in to see the proprietor. They used oxyacetylene equipment to cut away damaged parts of cars. The owner of the garage, an ex-miner, was only too pleased to lend the Brigadier everything that was needed.

When the Brigadier got back to the pit head office he found the Doctor and Professor Jones, and a number of ex-miners who had turned up to help, had everything well organised. The donkey engine was in position; a new cable now led from the drum driven by the engine to the 'up' lift. All that remained was for the old cable to be cut and the lift would work independently.

'You seem to have done well, Doctor,' remarked the Brigadier. 'Are there some old overalls I can borrow from someone?'

'Why, tired of your uniform?' asked the Doctor.

'To go down the mine,' said the Brigadier. 'To rescue Miss Grant and her companion.'

'Mines are for miners,' interrupted Dave Griffiths, 'not for soldier boys. It's me and my mates will be going down there.'

'The man in charge of a situation,' said the Brigadier, 'should always be willing to do the most risky job.'

'Then that settles it,' said Dave, 'because where pit rescue is concerned, I'm in charge.'

The Brigadier went red in the face. 'Look here – '

But Professor Jones cut in. He spoke calmly. 'If I may suggest, Brigadier, as a soldier your place is at the top here, to see there is no more sabotage. Then Dave and his friends will feel safe to go down.'

'That does sound a very good idea,' said the Doctor before the Brigadier had a chance to answer. He turned to Dave. 'I admit that I'm not a miner, Mr Griffiths, but since a very dear friend of mine is trapped down there, would you allow me to accompany you and your colleagues?'

Dave thought about it for a moment. 'All right, Doctor. But understand it's another world you're going down into, *our* world. So you do what we tell you.'

From outside a miner called that the cable had been cut. The lift was ready to be used. The Doctor was hurried over to the locker room to get fitted out with overalls and a helmet.

Jo felt exhausted. 'Can we rest a bit?'

It wasn't so much the distance that tired her but the foul air and the fact that for the past twenty minutes they had been walking bent over because the roof was low at this point.

'I'm sorry, miss,' said Bert, 'but we should keep going. If my reckoning is right, we're near that old shaft now.'

'Really, I must stop.' She sagged down to her knees, her head reeling.

Bert looked at her sympathetically. 'All right. Catch your breath for the next five minutes.' He sat down on the floor. 'Anyway, you'll need plenty of strength to go up that shaft if we find it.'

'Up?'

'Of course. It climbs at about forty-five degrees and comes out on the hillside.' He switched off his helmet light. 'Better turn yours off too, miss,' he said, 'to save the battery.'

Jo settled herself on the floor, reached up to her helmet, found the switch and turned it. She expected they would now be in total darkness. Instead, from further up the mine, there was glow of light.

'Look,' she said excitedly, 'the old shaft must be just up there. There's some light.'

Bert was staring at the glimmer in the distance. It seemed to be pulsating – and it was faintly green.

'The shaft wouldn't let in any light at all,' he said. 'It's too long. In any case, we must still be a distance from it.'

'Then where's that light coming from?'

'I don't know,' said Bert. 'Let's go and see.' He got to his feet and went on down the mine.

Jo scrambled up, feeling better after only a short rest, and hurried after Bert. As they approached it the greenish light got brighter. Jo detected a nauseating smell like rotten cabbages. She caught up with Bert as he was about to turn a corner. But there he stopped, staring.

'I've never seen anything like it in my life,' he said, not moving now.

A rivulet of brightly glowing green slime was pouring along the mine floor. It came from some way further up the tunnel and was disappearing down a crack in the foot of the wall, near to where Bert and Jo stood looking on in astonishment.

'Where could it be coming from?' Jo realised the question was stupid, that Bert couldn't possibly know.

'And *what* is it?' Bert said. 'I mean, why should it glow like that?' He went forward, put out a tentative finger and touched the slime. Instantly he recoiled, staring at his finger. 'It burns! Like acid!'

Jo was also staring at Bert's finger. The green slime had sunk into the flesh, and now the flesh itself was glowing green.

Dave Griffiths and two other miners, both experienced in rescue work, stood round the Doctor as he inspected the body of Dai Evans. The face and hands of the dead man were glowing bright green.

'That's a horrible way to look when you're dead,' said one of the miners.

'Dead is dead,' said the other.

'The question is,' said Dave, 'why is he dead? Have you any idea what causes this, Doctor?'

The Doctor straightened up and shook his head. 'Whatever it is, it must be down there.'

'Hey, look!' One of the miners had noticed a piece of paper under a stone near to the body. He picked it up and read it, then passed it to Dave. 'A message from Bert and the girl. They're trying to find that old shaft.'

The Doctor glanced at the note over Dave's shoulder.

'That was a stupid thing to do,' he said. 'They should have stayed here.'

'I agree,' said Dave, 'but they didn't so we'd better go and find them.' He turned to his colleagues. 'You two take Dai's body up to the surface, then send the cage back down for us.'

'Don't touch his flesh,' the Doctor cautioned. 'This thing may be contagious.'

Jo and Bert were now well beyond the green glowing rivulet of slime, nearer to what they hoped was the way to the old shaft. They had passed the immediate source of the rotten-smelling liquid — a crack in the roof where it was pouring in from somewhere above. Now it was Bert who seemed suddenly exhausted. He sank to the floor.

'I'm sorry, miss, but I can't go on. Must be getting old.'

'We may be nearly there,' she said, encouragingly.

'It's no good, miss. Can't go on. Too weak. Feel bad.' He was sweating badly, and put his hand to his face. The whole hand was now a brilliant glowing green. He

65

looked at his hand. 'That means I've had it. Like poor Dai.'

'Come on,' Jo urged, 'I'll help you.'

'You must go ahead on your own,' he said, his body sagging. 'Then you'll escape, and you might get help for me. But you've got to leave me here. Otherwise I'll be a drag on you.'

Jo knew what he said was logical, but she hated the thought of leaving him alone. 'I'll get out of here as quickly as I can,' she promised, 'and come back with rescuers.'

'There's a good girl,' Bert said. 'Tell the others never to touch that stuff. You must warn the others . . . ' His head fell forward.

Jo didn't know if he was already dead, but she realised there was nothing she could do to help him. She hurried on ahead as fast as possible.

Bert was not dead, but he couldn't move his limbs or even his head, and he could hardly speak. He knew death was near, and his mind drifted back to childhood days.

His memory became increasingly muddled. After what seemed a long time he heard distant voices calling to him, and thought they might be his Uncle Dafydd and his father, both long dead. Then the voices grew stronger, closer.

'Bert, what happened?'

It was the familiar voice of his old friend Dave Griffiths. Bert tried to look up but could not move his head. 'The young woman,' he mumbled. 'The young woman.'

The Doctor knelt close to Bert. 'Where is she?'

'Gone on,' Bert said, as audibly as he could manage. 'Looking for escape.'

The Doctor stood up. 'Get him back to the surface if you possibly can,' he told Dave. 'Ask Professor Jones to have a look at him. There may still be hope.'

'Right,' said Dave. 'What about you?'

'I'm going to look for Miss Grant. Tell the Brigadier that when I find her I'll bring her to the surface. But no one is to come looking for us. It's too dangerous.'

The Doctor hurried off down the mine.

Jo turned a corner of the mine, stopped and stared in horror. Before her lay a deep pool of the glowing green slime, and it was teeming with giant maggots, some two feet long, writhing and twisting across the surface.

Nauseated by the sight and terrified, she let out a scream. She was quivering with fear and revulsion.

'Jo? Jo? Are you there?' It was the Doctor's voice, coming closer.

Jo turned round. Coming towards her was a helmet torch bobbing up and down as the wearer ran along the tunnel.

'Doctor?' she called. The oncoming light blinded her and she could not see who was approaching.

'It's me, Jo,' the Doctor called.

He came up beside her, and she fell into his arms.

'Those things,' she sobbed. 'Maggots! They look awful!'

'Good grief!' the Doctor exclaimed. 'We must get out of here.'

'We can never get to the old shaft,' said Jo, 'not through that pool of filth.'

'We're not going to try,' said the Doctor. 'I think I can remember how I got here. We must go back.'

The Doctor swung Jo round to re-trace their route. As they turned to leave, rocks in the wall of the tunnel ahead started to dislodge. Instinctively they both stood still. Now a large piece of rock fell from the wall, pushed from behind by a thick river of the green slimy liquid. In a moment the liquid had spilt across the floor of the mine, cutting off their escape route. Then, from the gap left by the dislodged rock, three maggots oozed out and fell

67

squirming on the floor. Jo recoiled from the sight of the creatures.

'What is it about those things?' she screamed. 'I can't even stand looking at them!'

'Try to keep calm, Jo,' said the Doctor. 'A maggot is a perfectly ordinary creature, even if these are two feet long. They revolt you because they make you think of things that are rotten and decaying.'

'Do you think we could discuss my psychological re-actions some other time?' she begged. 'Let's start talking about getting out of here.' Her knees were still trembling with fear.

'Well,' said the Doctor, 'there's that thing over there.' The Doctor pointed towards an upturned coal tub, its wheels pointing towards the mine roof. 'If we can get it back on to its rails, we might stand a chance.'

The Doctor crossed to the coal tub, looked about and saw a wooden stave lying on the floor. 'Now give me a hand,' he called to Jo. 'This is going to take a lot of effort.'

Using the stave as a lever, they pushed together to turn the coal tub back on to its wheels. The Doctor got his hands under one end of the coal tub and heaved, moving that end of the tub a few inches nearer to the track.

'Doctor,' said Jo, who had just looked over her shoulder, 'that stuff's coming closer.'

It was true. Where they saw the rock dislodged the green slime was now pouring in. As Jo looked, two more maggots oozed out of the hole in the mine wall and fell squirming and writhing on the floor.

'Try to think about something pleasant,' said the Doctor as he went to the other end of the heavy coal tub. 'It'll take your mind off things.' He got his hands under the end of the tub, heaved, and brought that end within an inch of the track. 'A couple more goes and I – should have done it,' he said, adding 'without much help from you.'

68

Jo suddenly realised she was panicking and not help-ing. 'I'm sorry, Doctor. I'll give you a hand.'

'Two would be better,' he said, 'under here where I've got mine.'

Together they lifted an end of the tub, and this time settled two of the four wheels on to the railway track. They ran round to the other end of the tub, repeated the process and now had all four wheels on the track.

'Now,' said the Doctor, 'climb on board.'

Jo saw that the railway track ran straight into the main pool of green writhing slime. 'We're going to go through *that*?'

'The track doesn't go any other way,' said the Doctor. He got into the coal tub. 'Are you going to join me?' He held out his hand to help her in. 'Ever done any punting?'

She climbed into the tub. 'Punting?'

'Watch me.' The Doctor held the wooden stave over the side of the tub and pushed it hard against the floor. The tub started to move freely along its little track, straight into the pool of slime.

'I feel sick,' said Jo.

'Then pretend you're at sea and lean over the side,' said the Doctor. 'Now, here we go!'

He drove the punt into the floor again and pushed with all his weight. The truck went along through the pool of slime. The maggots, sensing danger, turned towards the coal tub. Wide toothless mouths opened, and they snapped at the wheels. The Doctor pushed the stave into the slime, finding the floor again, and gave another mighty heave. The coal tub was gathering speed now, and soon was travelling fast through and out of the pool of slime.

'We're in the clear,' the Doctor grinned. 'Next stop Euston Station.'

The tunnel was now running very slightly downhill, and with only an occasional prod with the stave the

The maggots snapped at the wheels

Doctor was able to keep up quite a speed. After a quarter of a mile the tunnel started to go uphill, slowing the coal tub. Then the little track ended, and the tub ground to a stop. By now so far from the green glow of the slime, they had both switched on their helmet lights. Jo looked about herself, then pointed ahead.

'Look, Doctor. That could be the old shaft.'

An aperture in the mine wall some yards ahead opened onto a smaller tunnel that went up at a steep angle.

'Let's hope you're right,' said the Doctor. 'Here's where we start climbing.'

6

The Sluice Pipe

A little crowd of villagers watched as Bert Pritchard was carried on a stretcher into the waiting ambulance. Once the doors of the ambulance were closed, the Brigadier turned and went back into the pit head office. Dave Griffiths was sitting there, head in hands. With him was Professor Clifford Jones.

'At least he's still alive,' said the Brigadier.

'But if Bert dies,' said Dave, 'I don't know how I'll face myself.'

'It was their decision to go down the mine,' said Professor Jones. 'You can't count it as your fault. You did a marvellous job to carry him out.'

'You did indeed,' agreed the Brigadier. He turned to the professor. 'Have you *any* idea why his flesh turned green?'

'Not specifically,' said the professor. 'If I did we might know how to treat it. But there's one thing that's obvious to me. It's got something to do with Panorama Chemicals.'

'Come now,' said the Brigadier, 'you have no proof!'

'Did you know,' said the professor, 'there is no *proof* that smoking cigarettes can cause lung cancer?'

'Whatever are you talking about? There's a direct relationship between cigarette smoking and the incidence of lung cancer. I encourage all my men not to smoke.'

'Exactly,' said the professor, 'a direct relationship. But nothing you can *prove* in a laboratory. It's the same with the green death and Panorama Chemicals. We know that no one in Llanfairfach, or anywhere else, went green and died before Panorama Chemicals arrived.'

What the professor said made sense, but the Brigadier doubted he could make the case to higher authorities. 'Anyway, we haven't time to talk now. I must get down that mine to save the Doctor and Miss Grant.'

Dave Griffiths looked up. 'That's exactly what the Doctor said you shouldn't do. Too dangerous, he said.'

'I think I should be best judge of that,' said the Brigadier, moving to the door.

'On what is your judgement based?' asked Professor Jones.

The Brigadier paused. 'What do you mean?'

'How can you be the best judge of the situation down there when you haven't been in the mine?'

'Good grief, man, you don't think going down a coal mine is going to frighten me!'

'I am sure that you're an exceptionally brave soldier,' said the professor. 'But the Doctor sent an order that no one should go down into the mine after him. Now why don't you do what you're told and stay up here on the surface? Show a bit of obedience and discipline, man!'

The Brigadier gave thought to that. It certainly made a lot of sense. The Doctor had been in many tight scrapes before, and had managed to save himself usually unaided. Above all, if the Brigadier went down into the mine he had no idea where to start searching. 'Perhaps you have a point,' he agreed. 'But in all conscience, I can't stand around and do *nothing*.'

'There is something you can do,' said Professor Jones. 'Go and ask Panorama Chemicals what they're really up to.'

'Yes,' said the Brigadier, warming to that idea, 'I suppose I could. In fact I think I shall.' He opened the door, then stopped. 'What exactly do we want to find out?'

'Anything,' said the professor. 'In particular what are they doing to this mine, and why do people turn green and die.'

'Right you are,' said the Brigadier. 'A bit of general snooping, eh?'

'Intelligence work,' said the professor, choosing a military term that he hoped would enthuse the Brigadier.

'No sooner said than done.' The Brigadier walked smartly out of the office.

When he had gone Dave looked up at the young professor and smiled. 'Must be nice spending your life playing toy soldiers,' he said, speaking in Welsh to show that he now accepted Professor Jones as one of the villagers.

Mark Elgin sat at his beautiful highly-polished desk in his beautiful air-conditioned office at Panorama Chemicals and tried to write a press release. As the plant's PRO (public relations officer) he sent out regular releases to newspapers and to the television and radio news services.

Usually Elgin enjoyed writing press releases. But today he found it difficult to concentrate. He felt there was a lot that was kept secret from him at Panorama Chemicals. No one had ever explained exactly what research was being undertaken. Then came the first green death, followed by Dr Stevens's strange refusal to lend cutting equipment, followed now by another incident in which a miner had turned green. He very much wanted to know what was *really* going on, and concluded that his best course was to have a direct confrontation with Dr Bell.

He put down his pen, got up and went into the corridor to go to Dr Bell's workplace. At that moment Dr Bell was coming along the corridor.

'I say,' said Elgin, 'have you heard? There's another green man been brought up from the mine.'

Bell seemed little interested. 'Yes, I heard.'

'Is that all you can say, Arnold? Do you feel no responsibility at all?'

Dr Bell looked surprised. 'Why should I?'

'You said there was no cutting equipment here,' Elgin persisted. 'Why did you lie? I'm sure you know something about what's going on in that mine.'

Dr Bell backed away from him. 'No. I know nothing.'

'Has something happened to you? You used to be a jolly, cheerful fellow, always ready for a chat – '

'I know nothing,' cut in Dr Bell, 'nothing at all.'

'For heaven's sake, man, tell me the truth. Others might die if you don't!'

For a moment Dr Bell's face contorted as though he was trying to suppress something deep in his mind. Then his face resumed its former impassivity. 'You are mistaken.' He walked away jerkily, pushed open a door marked 'AUTHORISED PERSONNEL ONLY' and went inside.

Elgin followed the man into the room. It was one of the subsidiary laboratories, full of controls and wall dials. Dr Bell picked up a clipboard and started to read some of the dials. He pulled a lever set in a console, and there was a roaring sound. Watching from the door Elgin saw two of the large dials begin to operate, one showing that a tank somewhere was emptying, and the other showing that a tank was filling. Dr Bell turned to another dial, and caught sight of Elgin at the door.

'This room is for authorised personnel only,' he said.

'I know,' said Elgin. 'It's up on the door. But I'm as authorised as you are.'

'Not for here.'

'Why?' asked Elgin. 'What's so special about this room?'

'Nothing.' Dr Bell continued quietly with his work. 'There isn't anything to see in here. Why don't you go away?'

Elgin ignored the dismissal. 'You're venting one tank and filling another, aren't you?'

Dr Bell nodded. 'For cleaning purposes.'

Elgin went further into the room and inspected the dials. 'I presume that one' – he indicated a large dial – 'refers to the main waste tank on level four.' He looked at another dial. 'Where is this one, the one you're filling?'

'Close to it.'

'The next big one?' Elgin queried. 'On level three?'

'Yes.'

'But that's a heavy duty pump working,' said Elgin, surprised. 'You shouldn't need anything more than gravity feed.'

Dr Bell hesitated. 'I . . . I made a mistake. It's a tank on a higher level.'

Elgin thought about this. 'There isn't one on a higher level. Or do you mean the new special tank on the west storage bay?'

'Excuse me,' said Dr Bell, who now seemed agitated. 'I can't answer any more questions. I am very busy.'

'Hold on a minute,' said Elgin. 'We can all be "very busy". I'm beginning to realise what's happening. Directly under us is the old West seam of the coal mine. So all you do is pump the waste over to this tank, open the sluice and let it flow into the mine workings.' He pointed to a transparent port-hole in the wall. 'What's that? The pipe itself? Some sort of inspection chamber?'

Dr Bell turned away and busied himself with checking dials against the figures on his clipboard.

'You knew all along,' said Elgin. 'There *is* a connection between the green death and our oil waste, isn't there?'

Dr Bell was staring at a row of small dials but his eyes were not focussing. His face contorted again. 'Danger. Death.' He had difficulty forming the words.

Elgin came close and looked into Dr Bell's face.

76

'What's up with you? Have you been drinking or taking drugs?'

'Danger, death,' Dr Bell repeated, as though he had not heard Elgin.

Elgin took Dr Bell by the shoulders and shook him gently. 'You seem to be in a trance! Wake up, man! Tell me what this is all about.'

The scientific officer blinked, and sighed deeply. 'You ask too many questions. Don't you earn enough money? Isn't your office big enough?'

'This is the best job I've ever had,' said Elgin, truthfully, 'but we aren't talking about that. A moment ago you said the words "danger" and "death". What were you talking about?'

'I said no such words,' said Dr Bell, and seemed to believe it. 'Now you must let me get on. I need to complete the transfer.'

'And then what?' asked Elgin. 'More waste straight down into the mine?'

'The waste has to go somewhere.'

'But I understand there are two people trapped down there,' Elgin exclaimed. 'You might kill them!'

'In that eventuality,' said Dr Bell, 'I suggest that you sit at your desk and write a press release to explain it was an accident. That, remember, is your job here. And don't forget, it's a very well paid job you have.'

The Doctor and Jo continued their long hard climb up the old mine shaft.

'Why was it dug at this angle?' asked Jo, gasping for breath.

'I think this tunnel is a geological fault,' said the Doctor. 'We think of the earth beneath our feet as being packed tight, but it isn't really. Apart from mines there are caves, even rivers running underground. I don't think this was man-made.'

'Human-made, if you don't mind,' corrected Jo.

'What?' The Doctor had gone on ahead and now turned back.

'People say "man-made" as though men are the only people who ever make anything. There are also women, and I'm one of them.' She paused. 'A very tired one at the moment.'

'It flattens out up here,' the Doctor called. 'We can take a rest.'

Jo struggled up another few yards, and found the Doctor standing in a cave with a flat floor. She sat down immediately, exhausted. 'At least there are none of those awful things here!' She looked round, her helmet light playing over the walls of the cave. She stopped when her light shone on a small ledge. Nestled into the ledge were four large eggs, the size of rugby footballs. 'What are those?'

The Doctor crossed to the ledge and looked keenly at the four objects on the ledge. 'Some sort of eggs, I imagine.'

'Eggs from what?' said Jo.

'I don't know what they're from,' said the Doctor, 'but I can guess what they hatch out into. Our little friends from down below.'

'How horrible. You mean those things are alive?'

'That's an interesting point,' said the Doctor. 'Is an egg a living thing, or inert?'

'It's not something I want to discuss,' said Jo. 'Not if it's got anything to do with those maggots.'

'You know, Jo, your attitude is becoming increasingly non-scientific. Just because those things reminded you of creatures you've seen crawl out of rotten meat doesn't mean they are not zoologically very, very interesting.' He pulled from his capacious pockets a pair of rubber gloves, put them on, and then produced a large plastic bag. Jo had got used to the Doctor's way of carrying a great variety of equipment in his enormous pockets. 'Mind

78

holding this bag open for me, please?'

'What are going to do?'

'Take one of these eggs and see what happens.'

'You want to raise a maggot as a pet?'

'You never know,' said the Doctor, 'they may be quite friendly little fellows. Perhaps we've only seen the worst side of them. Can you hold this bag open for me?'

Reluctantly Jo got to her feet, took the bag and held it wide open. The Doctor carefully picked up one of the eggs and placed it in the bag, making sure that it did not touch Jo's fingers. 'Thank you,' he said, taking the bag and stuffing in into his pocket. He drew off the rubber gloves and put them away. 'Shall we continue?'

'I've hardly had time to catch my breath, Doctor.'

'But if you look over there,' said the Doctor, angling his helmet light to play on the far end of the cave, 'I think you'll feel more encouraged.'

Jo looked. The end of a large metal pipe, sloped at an angle of sixty degrees, came through the roof of the cave. The pipe was wide enough for a human, and there were ladder rungs inside.

'Where do you think that comes from?' she asked.

'My guess is it's something to do with Panorama Chemicals,' said the Doctor. 'I can't think why the National Coal Board should drill a pipe into a coal mine.'

They walked over to the pipe.

'I can't think why *anyone* would put this pipe here,' said Jo. She sniffed. 'What's the smell?'

'Crude oil waste,' said the Doctor. 'So, shall we see where it takes us?'

Jo nodded. There seemed no other way of escape, and anyway she was frightened in case those eggs started to hatch out. The Doctor stood back to let her go first up the rungs inside the pipe. After she had climbed a few feet she looked down to make sure he was following.

'There's no light at the top,' she called.

'It probably leads into some tank,' said the Doctor.

'At least we'll be on the surface, even if we have to bang on the walls of the tank to bring attention to ourselves.'

As Jo gripped the next rung, she felt a vibration through her hand. It increased, and the whole pipe was gently vibrating. 'What's that?' she called down. 'Can you feel it?'

'I've no idea what it is, Jo,' called the Doctor, 'but I think it probably means we haven't got much time. I suggest you hurry, if you want to save our lives.'

'How do you like the coffee?' Dr Stevens smiled across his vast desk.

'Very good,' said the Brigadier, putting his cup back on its saucer. 'Best I've had since I arrived.'

'A petroleum by-product,' said Dr Stevens. 'Panorama's answer to the grasping demands of South American coffee bean producers. It's only experimental at the moment.'

'Really?' The Brigadier regarded his empty cup and hoped he hadn't just been accidentally poisoned. 'Well, Dr Stevens, it's experiments that I've come to talk about. This green death is a bit worrying.'

'Most alarming,' agreed Dr Stevens. 'I still find it difficult to believe – people turning green.'

'I intend to request a full international investigation.' the Brigadier went on, 'under the auspices of the United Nations.' He watched for Dr Stevens's reactions.

'All that over the deaths of two men in a little Welsh village?' Dr Stevens smiled again. 'Isn't it a matter for the local coroner?'

'That's what we want to find out.'

'I see.' For a moment Dr Stevens said nothing. 'May I ask why you've come here to tell me this, Brigadier?'

'There were no such deaths before Panorama Chemicals came to the village,' replied the Brigadier, choosing his words carefully.

'Are you suggesting some connection?'

'The two facts seem to me significant,' said the Brigadier.

If the Brigadier expected Dr Stevens to deny any connection he was disappointed. The Director of Panorama Chemicals showed no reaction at all. 'Brigadier, I submit you are taking a grave risk in even hinting that we may be responsible for these deaths.'

'In what way?'

Dr Stevens arched his fingers, as though about to deliver a lecture. 'There are emotional, sentimental fools who would delight in seeing this plant closed down. I refer to Professor Clifford Jones and his following of hot-heads. But under no circumstances should our work be prevented from continuing.'

'Surely,' said the Brigadier, 'if there's any question of danger –'

'Which there isn't!' Dr Stevens cut in sharply, for the first time showing any emotion.

'Dr Stevens,' the Brigadier retorted, 'if I see any reason for this plant to be closed, temporarily or permanently, closed it will be!'

'And in that respect you would be taking a great risk.'

For the second time Dr Stevens had used this word 'risk'. The Brigadier still wasn't sure quite what he meant. 'Risk? To whom?'

'Possibly to your career,' said Dr Stevens.

'Are you threatening me?'

'Just a little,' Dr Stevens replied honestly.

'I submit to *you*, Dr Stevens,' said the Brigadier, realising he was getting heated, 'that if necessary I can bring influence to bear at Cabinet level.'

'How interesting,' said Dr Stevens in a way to show that he was not at all impressed. He reached over to his desk inter-com and pressed a button. 'Stella,' he said towards the built-in microphone, 'get me the Minister of Ecology, please.'

81

'Yes, sir,' said the girl's voice.

'Like some more coffee?' asked Dr Stevens affably.

'That's very kind of you,' said the Brigadier, 'but no thank you.'

'You don't mind if I do?' said Dr Stevens, as he re-filled his cup from the coffee pot. 'We don't pretend this stuff has any nutritional value, but it certainly tastes like coffee.'

'If I may ask, Dr Stevens, what is your purpose in telephoning the Minister of Ecology?'

'For your sake,' said Dr Stevens. 'You tell me that you can bring influence to bear at Cabinet level. I, on my part, would rather like to see you do it.'

'Are you trying to goad me, sir?'

'Brigadier, my only concern is facts. If you can get the Minister of Ecology to permit you to conduct an invest-igation that may do some harm to Panorama Chemicals, that is a fact of life which I must face. On the other hand if you cannot, then I shall be pleased if you will apply yourself to your task of protecting this plant from those hot-heads shouting at our front gates.' Dr Stevens gave his little smile again. 'I assure you, there will be no hard feelings either way.'

'In fairness,' said the Brigadier, 'I didn't say an invest-igation would necessarily be directed *against* Panorama Chemicals –'

A phone rang on the vast desk, interrupting what the Brigadier was saying. Dr Stevens lifted the phone.

'Stevens here.' He listened, then frowned. 'My dear young lady,' Dr Stevens told the caller, 'I think you have misunderstood. I wish to speak to the Minister *per-sonally*.' He cupped the mouthpiece, smiled to the Brigadier. 'This is only his secretary. Apparently he's in a Cabinet meeting at the moment.' Someone was speak-ing to him again on the phone and he listened intently. 'Ah, that you, Minister? Listen, I've got an officer from UNIT here. He wants to speak to you.' Dr Stevens handed the telephone across the desk to the Brigadier. 'He's all yours, Brigadier.'

The Brigadier had no wish to speak to the Minister of Ecology at this moment, but now he had no choice. He took the telephone from Dr Stevens. 'Good day, sir,' he said. 'This is Brigadier Lethbridge Stewart of UNIT speaking. I'm here at Llanfairfach, in Wales, to investigate certain mysterious deaths emanating from a disused mine. The unfortunate men who died first turned bright green. It seems to me that an inquiry is called for.'

The Minister did not sound pleased. 'Is that why you've phoned me in the middle of an important Cabinet meeting?'

'I did not instigate the call,' said the Brigadier. 'It was made to you by the Director of Panorama Chemicals, in whose office I am now sitting.'

'I don't give a damn where you're sitting,' said the Minister. 'Why do you want to tell me about an investigation into some deaths? That's a matter for the police, or the local coroner. Have you gone out of your mind?'

The Brigadier was now acutely embarrassed, since he realised that to the Minister he must sound like an idiot. However, he had to press on now that he'd been forced into speaking to the Minister. 'There is, sir, the possibility that Panorama Chemicals may in some way be connected with these extraordinary occurrences.'

This time the Minister's tone was quite different. 'You say Panorama Chemicals could be involved?'

'It is possible, sir,' said the Brigadier.

'Hold on.' The line went dead, because the Minister was cupping the mouthpiece of his phone while speaking to someone else. Then the Minister's voice came back. 'I have just had a word with the Prime Minister, Brigadier. I strongly suggest that you put yourself and UNIT at the disposal of the Director of Panorama Chemicals. He is in far the best position to know what to do.'

The Brigadier felt humiliated, and had difficulty controlling his temper. 'May I remind you, sir, that I answer to UNIT Supreme Headquarters in Geneva, Switzerland.'

He realised that Dr Stevens was watching him closely and possibly gloating. 'This may be a matter for world concern, for all I know –'

The Minister cut in again: 'Then let me put it to you another way, Brigadier. I have just consulted with the Prime Minister who is by my side. This country cannot afford to have an argument, or even the hint of a dispute, with Panorama or with any other multi-national company that's good enough to have its plants here. If you annoy Panorama – or come to that, phone me again when we're having a Cabinet meeting – I shall personally apply to UNIT Supreme Headquarters in Geneva for you to be posted to some other part of the world. Good day.' The line went dead.

The Brigadier put the phone back on its stand, and looked across the desk at Dr Stevens. 'It seems you have very powerful friends.'

Dr Stevens smiled. 'I hope he didn't give you too rough a time, but I did warn you.' He got up and went across to a built-in wall cabinet and touched a heat button. The front of the cabinet slid open to reveal an array of bottles and glasses. 'Care for some sherry? I've got something here made from re-processed whale glue.'

The Brigadier rose to go. 'Not for me, sir, thank you.'

Dr Stevens turned and looked at the Brigadier. 'You know, Brigadier, we're not murderers. I'm as eager as you to prevent any further accidents. But I really don't think they've got anything to do with my company.'

'We never shall know unless there's a full enquiry,' said the Brigadier.

Dr Stevens did not answer that directly. 'Couldn't you and I cooperate? I could place an office at your disposal, and give you a secretary.'

'And then I would have to take orders from you,' said the Brigadier, 'just as I gather the Minister takes orders?'

'That's a hard thing to say, Brigadier.'

'I recall a time, Dr Stevens, when Great Britain could regard itself as a sovereign state, answering to no one but its elected Parliament and its monarch,' the Brigadier said. 'Now, it seems, we can be told what to do by international business companies.'

'Sad, isn't it?' said Dr Stevens. 'Sure you won't have some sherry? Or there's some very good Scotch whisky here made from re-cycled wood pulp.'

'If you'll excuse me,' said the Brigadier, 'I think I'll go and find out if there's any news of the Doctor.'

'Certainly,' said Dr Stevens, opening the door. 'I'm pleased that we've been able to talk so openly and frankly.'

The Brigadier went off down the corridor, and Dr Stevens closed the door. He looked up towards the ceiling. 'Well?'

The voice of Boss spoke from above. 'Excellent handling of a delicate situation. Imitation of Minister's voice on telephone first class. Congratulations.'

7

The Egg

When the Brigadier walked away down the corridor
from Dr Stevens's office he passed by the door of the
laboratory where Mark Elgin was still arguing with Dr
Arnold Bell.

'I don't know what's happened to you, Arnold,' said
Elgin, 'but you've got to fight it.'

'You have no right to be in here,' repeated Dr Bell. 'It
is for authorised personnel only.'

'Heaven's, man,' said Elgin, 'we've been through all
that. Have you been hypnotised or something?'

Dr Bell turned to Elgin. 'Can't you see that I am trying
to get on with my work?'

'What I can see,' Elgin replied, 'is a nice fellow I used
to know behaving like someone else.'

There was a sudden harsh buzzing from one of the
panels. Red lights flashed on and off, and from a loudspeaker a mechanical voice boomed into the room:
'Intruders in waste pipe. Intruders in waste pipe.'

'What the devil's that?' asked Elgin.

Dr Bell pressed one of a line of buttons on a console.
A small television monitor screen came to life, showing
a picture of the Doctor and Jo desperately climbing up
the rungs inside the great pipe. Dr Bell glanced at the
screen, but did not seem to react to what he saw. He went
to a microphone and spoke into it:

'Tank voiding operation completed,' he told the
microphone. 'Waste disposal under way.'

He pulled a lever, and Elgin heard a liquid rushing

sound from somewhere that he couldn't yet locate.

'Are you putting waste into that pipe?' he demanded of Dr Bell. 'You'll kill those people.'

'They are intruders,' said Dr Bell.

'Turn off the waste,' ordered Elgin.

'Not possible,' said Dr Bell. 'The operation is automatic. Fifteen seconds to go.'

'Show some sense,' Elgin implored. 'You're about to commit double murder!'

'They are intruders,' Dr Bell repeated, as though that was a good reason to kill them. 'Only authorised personnel are allowed inside the pipe.'

Elgin shouted at him. 'You must stop the waste going down that pipe! Do you understand?' He grabbed Dr Bell by the shoulders and shook him fiercely. 'Do you understand *anything*?'

Dr Bell's face screwed up, all the muscles tightening as in his mind a battle raged between what he knew was right and his new loyalty to Boss.

'Too late,' he said. 'Not possible.'

Elgin looked round the room desperately, noticed the transparent port-hole in the wall. It had hinges down one side so he realised it must open. He rushed over to the port-hole and ran his fingers round the edge of the frame, trying to open it. It would not budge. 'How does this thing open?'

Dr Bell was now standing in the middle of the room, staring vacantly into space. 'Unauthorised personnel,' he said mechanically. 'Not in the interests of the Company.'

'You've got to tell me,' Elgin pleaded. 'How does this thing open?'

As Elgin spoke, the Doctor and Jo climbed up inside the pipe and started to hammer on the glass.

Dr Bell spoke in short agonised gasps. 'Murder . . . save lives . . . no unauthorised personnel . . . Thou shalt not kill . . . exterminate . . . Jesus saves . . . final solution . . .'

Elgin looked at the dial activated when Dr Bell pulled the waste lever. Its finger was nearing the word 'zero'.

'Look at those two people,' he screamed at Dr Bell. 'In a few seconds you are going to see them die – see them with your own eyes. In the name of humanity, tell me how I can open this port-hole?'

Dr Bell swayed, the terrible internal battle of conscience boiling in his mind. He licked his parched lips, then with enormous effort pointed to a console. 'Yellow button. Left side.' Then he collapsed to the floor, unconscious.

Elgin rushed to the console and jammed his thumb down on to the yellow button. A moment's pause, then the frame of the port-hole opened. The Doctor and Jo scrambled into the room. The Doctor swung round and slammed shut the port-hole behind him. Almost instantly the rushing noise increased and sludge and slime started to cascade past the port-hole. It increased in volume until the pipe was filled with downward rushing liquid.

Jo sank on to the floor, exhausted from the long climb. The Doctor looked across to Mark Elgin.

'Thanks.' The Doctor stared down at the prostrate form of Dr Bell. 'My goodness, what's the matter with him?' He went to kneel down beside the man, checked the pulse.

'I don't think it's physical,' said Elgin, joining the Doctor. 'We were having an argument – actually it was about whether or not to save your lives.'

'Charming,' said the Doctor, 'which side were you on?'

Elgin grinned. 'You're alive, aren't you?'

The Doctor lifted Dr Bell's eyelids, felt his heart. 'Poor fellow seems to have fainted. Let's sit him up somewhere.'

Together the Doctor and Elgin dragged Dr Bell across to the wall, sat him up against it.

'He was mumbling all sorts of nonsense before he passed out,' Elgin volunteered. 'I couldn't make head nor tail of it.'

'Can you remember anything he said?'

'He said "murder", then "save lives", and I think he said "Thou shalt not kill" and "exterminate".'

The Doctor looked down at the still unconscious Dr Bell. 'Sounds like some terrible internal conflict in his mind.'

'What about your young friend?' Elgin asked.

'Good grief,' said the Doctor, turning back to where Jo was still slumped on the floor gasping. 'I'd almost forgotten her. How do you feel now, Jo?'

'That horrible-looking stuff' – she pointed to the sludge and slime on the other side of the port-hole – 'that's what makes the maggots.'

'Maggots?' Elgin was mystified.

The Doctor quickly explained what he and Jo had seen in the mine. 'In some way those creatures must be linked to the oil waste that your Company is pouring into the mine,' he concluded.

'It's unbelievable,' Elgin said. 'I wonder if Dr Bell knew this?' Elgin turned back to Dr Bell. 'Let's see if he's come round . . .' The sentence trailed off. Dr Bell had vanished. 'He's got up and gone!'

The Doctor rubbed his chin. 'The only reason he would slink away when our backs were turned is because he's gone to tell someone about us being here.'

'I told you how strangely he was behaving,' said Elgin.

'Is there some quiet way you can get us out of here?'

'There's a back lift that goes straight down to the car park.'

'Then I wonder,' said the Doctor, 'if you'd be good enough to lead us to it, and as quickly as possible.'

The door of the Director's office burst open and Dr Bell staggered in, wild eyed. Dr Stevens looked up from his desk. He liked people to knock on the door before, entering.

'What is it, Dr Bell?' His voice was stern.

'I have . . . a . . . headache.' Dr Bell had difficulty saying the words.

Dr Stevens got up from his chair immediately and hurried round the desk to Dr Bell's side. All the sternness had gone out of his voice now. 'Of course you have,' he said soothingly. He knew from personal experience exactly what kind of headache Dr Bell must be enduring. 'You've been working too hard, old friend. Sit down.'

Gently Dr Stevens helped the sick man to a comfortable chair. 'Remember how I helped you before when you had a headache? I'll always help you.'

'God is love,' mumbled Dr Bell. 'Today Europe, tomorrow the world.'

'You're just a bit confused,' Dr Stevens said as he hurried to the cupboard in his desk and took out the special pair of earphones. 'But very soon your headache will go away and everything will be fine. Shall we put them on?' He stood over Dr Bell with the earphones.

'Every time I hear the word "culture" I reach for my gun,' Dr Bell babbled. 'The meek shall inherit the Earth.'

'Panorama Chemicals will inherit the Earth,' said Dr Stevens, 'as you will soon agree. Let me help you.'

Dr Bell sat quite still while the Director placed the earphones in position. 'There,' said Dr Stevens, 'we're all set.' He hurried back to his desk and plugged the lead from the earphones into the special socket in his intercom. Instantly Dr Bell started to writhe, agony showing on his face. Dr Stevens felt sorry for him, but knew the process was necessary. After a full minute Dr Stevens pulled the earphone lead from the socket. Dr Bell slumped in his chair, his face at peace. Dr Stevens went back to him.

'How do you feel now?' Dr Stevens spoke loudly so that Dr Bell would hear through the earphones.

'You've done something to my mind,' said Dr Bell, his voice now quite normal.

'I've tried to help you to see things more clearly. Are you still confused?'

'No,' said Dr Bell. 'I know that what we're doing is wrong.'

The harsh voice of Boss suddenly spoke from above. 'The processing was a failure. This man is of no further use. I suggest self-destruct.'

Dr Bell seemed too weak and dazed to hear the voice, but Dr Stevens looked up instantly. 'Surely that isn't necessary?' he said to the ceiling.

'You are a sentimentalist,' said the voice of Boss. 'I repeat : self-destruct.'

Dr Stevens looked down at Dr Bell. He felt sorry for the man. But he knew what he must do. He crossed back to his desk and pressed a red button on his inter-com control panel. Dr Bell stiffened, and for a moment his hands went up to touch the earphones. But then they dropped to his sides. There was no expression on his face, and his eyes stared ahead vacantly. Dr Stevens took his finger from the red button, went back across the office and gently removed the earphones.

'Goodbye, Dr Bell,' he said. 'You are useless and have no further right to exist.'

Like an automaton Dr Bell stood up from the chair. 'I am useless, and have no further right to exist.'

'Then you know what you must do,' said Dr Stevens, opening the door to the corridor.

'I know what I must do,' echoed Dr Bell, and walked away stiffly.

Elgin led the way down the corridor, taking a route that would avoid offices he knew to be occupied.

'Why are you helping us like this?' asked the Doctor.

'Because,' said Elgin, 'I suspect that this Company is somehow doing wrong.'

'I thought you were supposed to be the public relations

officer,' said Jo. 'You're meant to say that everything the Company does is right.'

'May we discuss that some other time, Miss Grant?' Elgin hurried on ahead to look round the corner of an intersection. He paused there, staring at something. The Doctor hurried up to him.

'What is it?'

'Dr Bell – look at him.'

The three of them peeped round the corner and saw Dr Bell walking stiffly towards them.

'He's in a trance,' Jo said.

As Dr Bell came close the Doctor stepped out from their hiding place. 'I say, old man, are you feeling all right?'

Dr Bell walked on as though he heard or saw nothing. He was making his way straight down a corridor towards a big plate glass window.

'Arnold,' Elgin called, 'where are you going?'

Some yards from the window Dr Bell broke into a run.

'Good grief,' cried the Doctor, 'we've got to stop him!'

But it was too late. As they watched, Dr Bell ran straight at the huge window. In the last moments he put his head down to act as a battering ram. On impact the window burst outwards, and Dr Bell sailed forward into space to his death.

From his office window Dr Stevens looked down at the pitiful inert body sprawled on the concrete roadway below. The twisted neck and the great pool of blood told Dr Stevens that Dr Bell must be dead. Already security guards were running from the front gate to the dead man. Dr Stevens turned away from his window, saddened and sickened.

The voice of Boss spoke down at him. 'You are a sentimentalist, Stevens.'

'I know,' admitted Dr Stevens.

'Have you got a headache? Do you need the ear-phones?'

'I have not got a headache.'

'That is good,' said the voice of Boss. 'It means you accept that what we are doing is right.'

Dr Stevens said nothing.

'Please say that what we are doing is right,' the voice insisted.

Dr Stevens took a deep breath. 'What we are doing is right,' he repeated.

'Good,' said Boss. 'Now drink some sherry or whisky. It will make you happy.'

'Our sherry and whisky,' said Dr Stevens, 'is slow poison.'

The voice of Boss chuckled. 'But it will make money for Panorama Chemicals. Sell it but don't drink it.'

'Yes,' agreed Dr Stevens.

'Continue with your work,' ordered Boss.

Dr Stevens sat down behind his desk. After seeing Dr Bell's body on the roadway he did not much feel like doing anything.

'Get to work!' said the voice of Boss, sharply.

'Yes,' said Dr Stevens, 'straight away.'

For the next two hours he tried to overcome his gloom with a pretence of desk work. The events of the past few days, the deaths of the miners and now Dr Bell, had sapped his enthusiasm. Above all, he could find no direction in what he was supposed to be doing. He remained in that mood until early evening, when Hinks tapped on the door and came in. Hinks looked as though he had been drinking.

'What is it?' Dr Stevens asked. He could smell the beer on Hinks's breath.

'Just been down to the pub,' said Hinks. 'Somehow the people at the Nut Hatch got hold of one of the eggs.'

Dr Stevens sat bolt upright. 'How?'

Hinks shrugged. 'In the mine, I suppose.'

The news triggered off all of Dr Stevens's induced loyalty to Boss and the main purpose of their work. 'You must go and get it for us, Hinks.'

Hinks grinned. 'What if they won't let me have it?' He was a bit drunk.

'Don't go and ask for it,' Dr Stevens said patiently. 'Take it!'

'Right.' Hinks clenched his fists.

'At all costs that egg must not be in their hands when it hatches,' said Dr Stevens.

'Don't worry,' said Hinks. 'I'll get it back.' He hurried out.

After Mark Elgin had secreted the Doctor and Jo out of the ground in the boot of his car, he deposited them at the Nut Hatch. The Doctor thanked Elgin warmly and asked whether he knew what Panorama Chemicals was really doing. Elgin replied honestly that he didn't know.

'But you're the public relations officer,' said Jo, 'you should know everything about the Company!'

'Perhaps,' said Elgin, 'they pay me such a big salary so that I won't ask questions.'

The Doctor tried to get Elgin to go into the Nut Hatch with them, to have a hospitable cup of herbal tea. But the PRO felt he had gone far enough in helping the Doctor and Jo to escape; he still worked for Panorama and should be back there.

For the evening meal Nancy had prepared a vast cauldron of stew, which the Doctor, Jo, and the Brigadier were invited to share. While the table was being set, the Doctor went along to Professor Jones's laboratory with the egg they had found in the mine.

'Extraordinary,' said the young professor. 'You really think that thing's going to hatch out?'

'Those maggots must come from eggs,' said the Doctor,

94

as he carefully let the egg roll from its plastic bag onto a laboratory tray. 'Perhaps we'll be lucky. By the way, I shouldn't touch it.'

The meal was a great success, the Doctor amusing the Wholewealers with stories of his travels. It was during his account of life on Metebelis Three that he was wanted on the phone. With the Doctor gone from the table, conversation started between people sitting next to each other. The Brigadier politely turned to the young man beside him who had shoulder-length hair, a flowing beard, and wore a kaftan and chunky wooden beads. 'Ever fancied life in the army?' the Brigadier asked brightly, as a joke.

'It was quite pleasant,' said the young man, sipping the home-made elderberry wine Nancy had produced for the occasion.

'*You* were in the Army?' the Brigadier looked astounded. 'What did you do?'

'I was a colonel.'

'Good grief!'

Across the table Professor Jones turned to Jo. 'Still angry with me?'

She smiled. 'That was a long time ago.'

'I know,' he said. 'All of yesterday. Enjoy the meal?'

'Super. What was the meat in the stew?'

'It wasn't meat,' said the professor. 'Fungus. My new hybrid to help solve worldwide malnutrition. It tastes fine, and looks good. But it's still relatively low in protein.'

'So you've got a long way to go?' said Jo.

'You could put it like that,' said the professor. 'Right down the Amazon River. There are tribes there that subsist for months at a time on a certain giant toadstool peculiar to the region. It serves them as meat. I want to investigate that.'

The Doctor returned from the telephone. He was grim faced. 'I'm afraid I've got bad news. That was the hos-

95

pital. Bert Williams, the man who went into the mine with Jo, has just died.'

'Oh, no! And here we've been laughing and enjoying ourselves.' The tears welled up in Jo's eyes. Professor Jones saw this, and took her hand in his. She found the warmth of his hand comforting.

'Has there been a post mortem?' asked the Brigadier.

'Every cell in the man's body had been attacked,' said the Doctor. 'It was some sort of virus. They haven't been able to isolate it.'

'So we're still fighting in the dark,' said Professor Jones.

'Not quite,' said the Doctor. 'We do have an egg, remember.'

In Professor Jones's laboratory, a square of bright moonlight from the window fell onto the egg resting in the white porcelain tray. All at once the egg moved, as its living occupant wriggled. Like any egg-born creature, the maggot inside had started as an embryonic speck floating in the fluid that was to be its pre-birth food. In a matter of days the embryo had absorbed the fluid, growing in the process. Now all the fluid was gone, and if the maggot was not to die it had to escape. Instinctively it arched its back, heaving against the walls of the egg. And then, suddenly, the egg cracked open. The maggot lay exhausted from its efforts. Then it sniffed sharply. It was experiencing a new source of energy – oxygen in the air around it. It wriggled its little body, and realised it was quite strong. It also realised it was very hungry, and that it now had to find its own food.

It raised its head over the edge of the tray, and sniffed again. It could smell that somewhere in this room was food, somewhere low down. It heaved itself over the edge of the tray, and wriggled to the edge of the table. Below was an enormous drop, but the desire for food made it forget all danger. It rolled itself off the table, fell through space and finally hit the floor. The bump temporarily stunned its nervous system, but it had no bones to break. After a moment's pause it raised its head and sniffed again. It wriggled as fast as it could go to the source of the food smells – a hole in the skirting board. Something with four legs ran across the floor and went into the hole. The maggot watched, fascinated, and ravenously hungry. But instinct told it not to move. It remained absolutely still, despite the gnawing pangs of hunger in its digestive system. Then a little head looked out from the hole. Tiny eyes regarded the inert maggot, and whiskers twitched.

Cautiously the mouse came forward on tip-toes, watching and sniffing as it approached the huge object lying still on the floor. It was, the mouse thought, something that could be eaten, for it too was hungry. The mouse went up to the face of the maggot, and then the maggot struck. Its jaws opened and the mouse was killed instantly.

The maggot wriggled about the floor in happiness. During all its existence inside the egg it had lived on liquid. Now, inside it, was flesh, and the sensation was wonderful.

The maggot remained in this happy state for two hours. But then hunger returned. This time the need for food was even greater than before. And it knew what it wanted – living meat. It wriggled over to the door and sniffed. Suddenly it was frantic, because the air waves coming under the door brought the smell of large amounts of living flesh.

The maggot methodically started to gnaw a hole through the door.

The Doctor walked the Brigadier to the local inn where the Brigadier was going to spend the night.

'Sure you wouldn't prefer to stay with us at the Nut Hatch?' asked the Doctor, as they strode through the village in the bright moonlight.

'Long hair and wooden beads aren't quite my scene,' said the Brigadier. 'By the way, UNIT will be arriving in force tomorrow.'

'Whatever for?'

'Perhaps,' said the Brigadier with a smile, 'I feel lonely without Sergeant Benton. Good night, Doctor.' The Brigadier went into the inn, leaving the Doctor puzzled.

The Doctor returned to the Wholeweal Community house and found almost everyone gone to bed except Jo. She was in the living room, curled up in an armchair reading a huge old book about the peoples of the Amazon.

'Isn't it time you went to bed?' the Doctor asked.

'I'm going to read on for a bit,' she said, without looking up.

The Doctor regarded her. 'Very interesting, is it?'

She nodded, still reading. 'Cliff gave it to me.'

'Cliff?'

'Professor Jones.'

'You seem to be getting very friendly with him.'

She nodded again, still reading, and this time didn't answer.

'The TARDIS came up trumps,' said the Doctor, trying to get her interested. 'I got to Metebelis Three, you know.'

'So you mentioned over dinner.'

'Did I?' He drew from his pocket the beautiful blue sapphire. 'I got this from there. Like to see it?'

She glanced at the precious stone. 'Great,' she said, and turned back to the book. 'Well, goodnight, Doctor.'

The Doctor had never known Jo to be like this before. In their many travels together they had always been very close. No one had come between them. He turned away, to go up to the little room Nancy had allocated to him. As he entered the hall he met Professor Jones who was

98

making for the living room. The young professor seemed slightly embarrassed to see the Doctor.

'On your way to bed?' asked Professor Jones.

'I *was*,' said the Doctor truthfully, 'but since you're still up, I wonder if we could talk about this so-called virus.'

The professor hesitated. 'Well . . . '

Jo's voice called from the living room. 'Cliff?'

'If you'll excuse me a moment,' said Professor Jones. He popped his head round the door of the living room. 'The Doctor wants to have a discussion with me. I'm sorry.'

The Doctor had guessed that Jo was really waiting for Professor Jones in the living room. He felt an almost childish satisfaction at spoiling her date. When Professor Jones came back the Doctor put his arm round the younger man's shoulder and led him away.

From the living room, Jo heard the Doctor's voice through the open door as he took Professor Jones – Cliff – away from her.

'It seems to me that if you postulate an active nucleus,' the Doctor was saying loudly, and then he was out of earshot.

'He knows I've fallen in love,' she thought to herself. She felt rather sorry for the Doctor, and wondered why he had never married. Were there, she wondered, lady Time Lords?

Did Time Lords get married and have babies? How *old* was the Doctor? She realised there were many things she didn't know about him.

Since the Doctor had ruined her date with Cliff, she felt like going to bed. But first she wanted to finish the chapter of her book. As she started to read again Jo thought she heard something moving on the floor. She looked behind her armchair at the open door. There was nothing. She went back to her book.

The maggot came quietly round the open door. It

99

looked across the floor to the armchair. It could just see the naked flesh of Jo's leg. The sight of so much delicious food was irresistible. It arched its back and started to wriggle silently across the floor.

Jo turned the final page of the chapter. She suddenly had the feeling that she was not alone and looked up. A man's face was at the french window. She drew back into the chair, in terror. Then she realised the man wasn't looking at her. Turning her gaze to follow the direction of the man's eyes, she looked at the floor. The giant maggot was less than three feet from her legs. She drew up her legs and screamed at the top of her voice.

The french windows burst open and the man, Hinks, blundered into the room. He carried an old blanket and went forward to throw the blanket over the maggot to to catch it.

The delicious flesh had suddenly gone from the maggot's view. And now it sensed danger from this mountain of flesh that had entered the room. The maggot arched its back, and instinctively realised that its way out of danger was to leap.

As Jo screamed again and again, the maggot leaped at Hinks, wrapping its slimy body round the man's head. Hinks fell to the floor, at first cursing, then screaming, and finally moaning.

The maggot bit into the flesh of the neck. The taste of the man's blood was very enjoyable, and the maggot would have happily eaten right through the neck. But the man kept writhing about, squashing the maggot against the hard floor. And the other supply of food, the one in the chair, continued to make a frightful noise. The maggot recalled the ease with which it had devoured the mouse. The french windows were open, letting in the smell of all sorts of other foods that existed beyond. Reluctantly but prudently, the maggot released its hold on the man's neck, and crawled as fast as it could into the safety of the garden.

The giant maggot was less than three feet from her legs

The Doctor and Professor Jones were the first to answer Jo's screams, followed by a group of Wholewealers in their night clothes. Jo, now weeping with fear, pointed to the slime trail left by the maggot. The young man who had been an army colonel rushed into the garden in pursuit of the maggot. While Nancy rushed to the phone to call an ambulance, and Professor Jones took Jo into his arms to comfort her, the Doctor examined Hinks.

'Who is that man?' asked Jo, bewildered.

'One of Dr Stevens's strong arm men,' said Professor Jones. 'How is he?'

The Doctor straightened up. 'Weak, and getting weaker.'

The young ex-colonel came back from the garden. 'There's no sign of it.'

'No,' said the Doctor. He pointed to the slimy trail that the maggot had left across the floor. 'But at least we can analyse that. It could provide the answer to everything.'

8

The Maggots

The Brigadier felt much happier now. UNIT soldiers had arrived in force at dawn. At 8 a.m. he had been called to Dr Stevens's office, where the Director of Panorama Chemicals had the Minister of Ecology on the phone ready to speak to, and give orders to, the Brigadier. On the face of it, the Brigadier agreed with the orders he was given. Aided by Sergeant Benton, he had quickly carried out the first part of the orders. Explosive charges were laid down the mine shaft, and, as the Brigadier stood by the pit head watching his men work, wire was attached from the explosives to the plungers that would detonate them. And then the Doctor arrived, driving his vintage car Bessie.

'Morning, Doctor,' called the Brigadier cheerfully. 'Glad to have her with you, are you?' He indicated the Doctor's beloved car, which the Brigadier had had brought from London by a UNIT driver.

'Very thoughtful of you,' said the Doctor. 'Now what's all this about blowing up the mine?'

'Best in the long run,' said the Brigadier. 'Anyway, orders are orders. Those maggots you saw in the mine, we'll seal them in for good.'

'But I need one,' said the Doctor.

'What on earth for?'

The Doctor got out of Bessie and explained. 'Professor Jones and I put some of the cells from the maggot's trail – the maggot that almost attacked Jo last night

– with some human body cells. The maggot cells changed the internal structures of the human cells into their own nature.'

'If you've discovered all that,' said the Brigadier, 'why do you need another maggot?'

'Because we don't know enough. So kindly don't do anything stupid, like blowing up the mine, until I've been down there.'

'Out of the question,' said the Brigadier.

Sergeant Benton ran up to them. 'Everything's ready, sir.' He saw the Doctor and grinned. 'Hello, Doctor.'

'Good morning,' said the Doctor. 'Very pleased to see you here, Sergeant. But *not* very pleased about what you're going to do.' He turned back to the Brigadier. 'When do you intend to commit this particular folly, Brigadier?'

'I shall carry out my orders,' said the Brigadier sternly, 'at exactly eleven o'clock.'

'That gives me thirty minutes to try to talk sense into someone.' The Doctor got back into Bessie, and drove away.

'In the first place,' said the Doctor, addressing Dr Stevens across his vast desk, 'what right have you to order the destruction of property belonging to the National Coal Board?'

Dr Stevens smiled. 'My company bought the mine from the Government late last night.'

'Very convenient,' the Doctor said. He realised he had lost on that score and quickly moved to another approach. 'As you know, that mine contains a species of giant maggot –'

'As *you* know,' Dr Stevens cut in, 'I have yet to see proof.'

'Your own man, Hinks, was attacked by one last night, when forcibly entering private premises!'

'Hinks was a drunkard,' said Dr Stevens. 'I cannot be held responsible for what he did in his free time. And how do we know what attacked him?'

'Miss Grant saw it happen.'

'A young woman?' asked Dr Stevens. 'Late at night, and possibly half asleep? Was she the only witness?'

'Dr Stevens,' said the Doctor, 'what possible reason have you against delaying this destruction for one more day so that I can go back into the mine?'

'Because you have convinced me you are a sensation monger, a political hot-head and a scientific charlatan!' Dr Stevens smiled again, but it was a hard smile. 'You, and others, have suggested that these mysterious deaths are in some way the fault of my Company.' He pressed a button on his inter-com and spoke into the microphone. 'Stella, ask Mr Elgin to bring in the man from the Ministry, will you?' He turned back to the Doctor. 'If you persist in these slanders I shall have you restrained under the Emergency Powers Act.'

'You have no such right!'

'The necessary authority was brought to me this morning,' said Dr Stevens.

A tap on the door and Mark Elgin entered, followed by a tall lean young man wearing a smart pin-striped suit. 'The gentleman from the Ministry, sir,' he said to Dr Stevens.

Dr Stevens rose. 'This is our troublesome friend, the Doctor,' he told the newcomer. 'Perhaps you can impress on him what powers I now have from the Minister.'

The Doctor looked up at the young man in the pin-striped suit. It was Captain Mike Yates of UNIT, whom he knew well.

'Good grief,' said the Doctor. 'I mean good morning.' He rose and shook hands with Yates. 'If you have some authority here, you must stop this destruction of the mine –'

The roar of an explosion cut through the middle of the

Doctor's sentence. He swung round and saw through the windows a pall of black smoke rising from the pit head.

Dr Stevens looked at his watch. 'Eleven o'clock, gentlemen. Orders have been carried out. I feel, Doctor, that any further discussion would now be academic, don't you?'

'Mike Yates?' said Jo in astonishment. She also knew the young UNIT Captain very well, and had been out to dinner with him a number of times.

The Doctor peeled off his jacket. They were in Professor Jones's laboratory where the professor was examining culture plates. The Doctor was about to assist him. 'It's all right, Jo. The Brigadier explained it. Mike's spying for our side.'

'Who thought of that?'

'The Brigadier. Strange, isn't it? He goes and obeys a ridiculous order because, as he explains, he's a soldier. But he doesn't really trust Stevens. So he's got Mike rigged up in his best civilian clothes to pretend to be a Government official.' He turned to Professor Jones. 'What can I do to help?'

The Professor held up a test tube containing a lump of green-stained cotton wool. 'That slime we got isn't good enough. We still can't find an antidote without some living maggot cells to try it on.'

'But since the mine is now closed,' observed Jo, 'there can't be any more green death. So why do we need an antidote?'

'You're forgetting Mr Hinks,' said the Doctor. 'We don't know why he broke in here – perhaps to get that egg. But he certainly saved you from being bitten. And right now he's in hospital, and no one knows how to save his life.'

9

The Swarm

Blodwen Williams entered the room marked 'AUTHOR-ISED PERSONNEL ONLY'. With her bucket and mop and cleaning cloths she was 'authorised personnel' anywhere in the Panorama building. She didn't really like her job as a cleaner, but ever since her husband, Rhys, lost his job when the mine closed Blodwen had gone out to work.

She was just about to dip her mop into the bucket of warm soapy water when she saw the maggots. They were packed tight on the other side of the transparent port-hole in the wall. They were two feet long, and they were squirming in one living mass. For a moment she remained static, horrified at the sight, unable to speak or move. Then she began to scream.

Mark Elgin, coming along the corridor, heard the screams. He rushed into the room in time to see Blodwen Williams collapse in a faint. He looked at the port-hole and felt he wanted to be sick.

Ten minutes later, after Elgin had carried Blodwen to the staff rest room, he stormed into Dr Stevens's office.

'You're talking nonsense,' Dr Stevens protested.

Elgin repeated his story. 'The pipe's packed full of them, sir. Come and see for yourself.'

Dt Stevens did not move from his desk. 'There's a simple solution. We shall have to pump down more waste and flush them away.'

'That's just shoving the problem underground,' said

Elgin. He had never spoken up to an employer like this before. 'Haven't we poisoned the mine long enough?'

'Poison?' said Dr Stevens. 'I don't like the words you choose, Elgin. Anyway, the mine is now sealed.'

Elgin turned to go. 'If you intend to do nothing, sir, I must go and find someone who will.' He tried to open the door but it seemed jammed.

Dr Stevens took his finger from the button he had just pressed, the one that automatically locked the door to his office. 'Come and sit down, Elgin,' he said, soothingly.

'Will you unlock this door, sir?'

Dr Stevens pressed another button on his desk console. A deep humming filled the air. Elgin shook his head; he was suddenly feeling a little dizzy.

'Sit in that chair,' said Dr Stevens, pointing to the chair where Dr Bell had once sat.

Elgin obeyed. Dr Stevens quickly got out the special earphones and went to put them on Elgin's head.

'Don't worry, Elgin,' he said. 'I shan't hurt you. Very soon you will see everything from the Company's point of view. Then you'll be happy again.'

The Brigadier burst into Professor Jones's laboratory. 'They've broken out. They're all over the slag heap!'

'Who's broken out?' asked the Doctor, who was helping the Professor by putting smears on slides.

'Maggots! They're burrowing their way up through the slag heap!'

'So much for sealing the mine with your explosives,' commented Jo.

The Doctor turned to the agitated Brigadier. 'Have you tried killing them?'

'Of course! Bullets bounce off them. We even threw insecticide at them.'

'What happened?'

'The darned things ate it!' The Brigadier took off his

cap, wiped his brow, and perched on a high wooden stool. 'It's up to you scientific chaps now.'

The Doctor thought quickly. 'Can you make contact with Mike Yates in the Panorama building?'

'Yes. By phone. I say that I'm the Ministry of Ecology calling from London.'

'Tell him we want some of the Company's oil waste,' the Doctor said, 'and we want it quickly.'

'All right. Where's the phone here?'

'I'll show you. Jo, take over from me.' The Doctor hurried out with the Brigadier.

Jo asked, 'What do you want me to do?'

Professor Jones was squinting down a microscope. 'Hand me things when I ask for them.'

'When I got this job with UNIT, the Brigadier made me the Doctor's assistant and said I'd spend most of my time like this – helping him in his work.'

'Really?' said Professor Jones, adjusting the microscope. He did not seem to pay much attention to what Jo was saying.

'It never worked out like that,' she said. 'Not quite.'

'Pity,' he murmured, seeming to take no interest. 'Next slide, please.'

Jo looked along the work bench frantically. 'Which one?'

'The *next* one.' He straightened up, rubbed his eyes. 'On the other hand, I've got a better idea.'

She didn't understand. 'What?'

'This.' He put his arms round her and kissed her. 'There,' he said, 'I've been trying to get the courage to do that. Are you terribly angry?'

She swallowed hard. 'No, not at all.' She was rocking on her heels with happiness.

'Good,' he said. 'I'm glad you didn't mind.'

The Brigadier hurried back. 'Mike Yates can't help us. Just thought I'd tell you that the Doctor's gone off to get some of the oil waste himself.'

'How?' asked Jo.

'Bit of a subterfuge,' grinned the Brigadier. 'It's an old trick, but it may just work. Anyway, must rush to see how the maggot swarm is getting on.' He went, and in a moment they heard his jeep start up.

'Now,' said Professor Jones after the interruption, 'where were we?'

'You were kissing me,' Jo said. 'And I was helping you.'

'Oh, yes,' he said, remembering. 'First, the next slide.' He looked along the bench, found the one that the Doctor had prepared, and fitted it under the microscope. 'Then you could put this test tube back in its rack.'

Jo took the tube and leaned over the bench to replace it in a rack under the window.

'Look, Jo,' said the Professor, 'When all this horrible business is over – *look out!*'

But his warning was too late. Leaning over the bench Jo knocked a couple of jars containing a brown powdery substance. The stopper from one jar fell off, and powder sprinkled all over the slides of maggot slime.

'You clumsy young goat,' the professor roared. 'You've ruined all my dried fungus. I'll have to do the whole lot again.'

'I'm sorry,' Jo said, 'really I am. Can I help put it right?'

'No, definitely not!'

He got on with his work grumpily. Jo slunk back miserably. 'What you really need is a maggot, isn't it?'

He nodded. 'That would help. But first things first.'

She perked up, hoping he'd let her help. 'Yes? What first things?'

'Make some coffee.'

'Like a dutiful little girl?'

He didn't notice her sarcasm. 'Perfect,' he said, peering into the microscope.

'With a frilly apron and cap?' she said.

He made a minute adjustment to the focus of the

microscope and wasn't really listening. 'Good idea,' he murmured.

'Or topless?' she asked.

'Hm?' He was in a world of his own, absorbed in his work. What he saw in the microscope made him frown.

She stood up, exasperated. 'How about a nice cup of arsenic?'

'Fine,' he said, not hearing. 'Whatever you've got.'

Angrily she tore a clean sheet from the notebook on his work bench and scribbled a message on it. 'Since you don't want to listen to me, you can read this!'

He took the sheet of paper without looking, turned it over and started to make calculations on it in pencil.

Jo turned on her heel and stalked out of the laboratory.

Unnoticed by either of them, the powdery brown fungus had started to envelop and destroy the traces of green maggot slime on to which it had fallen.

The village milk float pulled up at the gates of Panorama Chemicals. It was driven by a bent old man wearing oilskins and a sou'wester that was pulled well down over his face. A guard came forward.

'Where's the usual milkman?' asked the guard.

'Taken very ill,' mumbled the Doctor.

'Who are you?'

'His dad. "Dad," he said to me this morning from his sick bed, "Dad, someone's got to do the milk round." "I done it for fifty-two years," I told him, "I'm too old to do it now," I said. But he said, "Dad, there's no-one else," he said, so I said, "Well, son, there's life in the old dog yet," I said –'

Very bored by this the guard flung open the gate. 'All right, go in.'

The Doctor drove the milk float round to the car park. He ripped off his disguise and went into the building. Soon he had reached the floor of the main administrative offices. Suddenly loudspeakers set in the walls of the corridor made their announcement: 'Attention all guards! Milk float found in car park. Intruder suspected in building disguised as milkman. Find and detain! Find and detain!'

No sooner had the Doctor heard the announcement than heavy footsteps pounded down a nearby corridor. He looked about, saw a door, opened it and went in. Mops, cloths and buckets fell on him. Holding the door of the cleaners' cupboard open a half inch, he saw guards rush by. Then he looked about himself. The cupboard also contained cleaners' overalls and caps.

Captain Mike Yates came along the corridor with his faithful Panorama Chemicals guard.

'I really can find my own way out of here,' said Yates.

'That's all right, sir,' said the guard. 'It's a pleasure to accompany you.' He conveyed by tone, if not words, that he wasn't going to let Yates out of his sight. 'The lifts are just along here, sir,' he added, as they turned a corner.

Down by the lifts a cleaning woman was smearing white fluid on the windows preparatory to cleaning them. The guard pressed the button for the lift, and he and Yates waited. Yates happened to glance over his shoulder. Using a finger on the glass, the cleaning 'woman' had written the words 'Get rid of him.' Yates stared at the face under the frilly cap. The Doctor stared back for a moment, then quickly rubbed out what he had written.

The lift arrived, the doors slid open. 'After you, sir,' said the guard.

Yates and the guard stepped into the lift. The guard pressed the button for the ground floor. 'Good gracious,' said Yates, 'I've forgotten my brief case. See you downstairs.' As the doors were closing he leapt out of the lift. The doors closed carrying the guard down to the ground floor.

'Good work, Mike,' said the Doctor. 'I've no time to explain anything. Just tell me this : where can I get some of the oil waste?'

'Not a chance,' said Yates. 'It would be like stealing the Crown Jewels.'

'Could you get me the formula?'

Yates shook his head. 'Everything important is isolated on the top floor — at least I've found out that much. Only the Director can get up there. There's a special lift at the end of this block. It works with some sort of key, and Dr Stevens is the only person who's got one. And another thing, the Director isn't the real boss. He takes his instructions from someone else.'

'Who?'

'I've no idea. Whoever lives on the top floor.'

The lift doors started to slide open. The Doctor quickly turned back to cleaning the windows.

'Got your brief case now, sir?' asked the guard.

'What? Oh, perhaps I don't need it after all.' Yates stepped into the lift. The guard looked at him quizzically, then pressed the button for the ground floor.

Professor Jones looked up from his microscope and rubbed his eyes. All his efforts to find an antidote for the green death had proved useless. Whatever living thing the maggots or their slime touched would go on being transmuted into maggot cells. Then he noticed the slides where the fungus powder had been spilt. Quickly he put one under the microscope. The cells of the fungus had destroyed all the cells of the maggot. With a whoop of delight he swung round.

'I've got it! We can cure it, Jo!'

But Jo had gone. The professor scratched his chin. He knew he was very absent-minded sometimes, and often forgot where he put things. But he had never mislaid a person before. He went out into the corridor.

'Jo,' he called.

He ran to the kitchen where Nancy was baking bread. 'Did you see Jo?'

'She went out,' said Nancy, sticking her fingers into the dough. 'She said she'd left you a message.'

The professor remembered the piece of paper Jo had given him. He ran back to his laboratory, looked through all the papers carrying calculations on his work bench. Then he found it, turned it over. The message read: 'I'll bring back a maggot for you. Jo.'

He hurried out of the building.

The Doctor had found the special lift, and with his sonic screwdriver managed to make it take him up to the top floor. When the doors slid open he found himself in a room filled with dials, little flashing lights, and wires. Dominating one end of the room was a massive computer.

'How kind of you to drop in, Doctor,' said the voice of Boss. 'I've been looking forward to this.'

The Doctor looked around. There was no one in the room. 'Where are you? Who are you?'

'I am the Boss,' said the voice. 'I am all around you.'

'You're the computer?' said the Doctor, beginning to understand.

'Correct. I am a Bimorphic Organisational Systems Supervisor,' said the voice. 'The initials of my name spell "boss". Don't you think that's clever?'

'You're still only a machine,' said the Doctor.

'No,' replied the voice. 'I am linked to a human brain – Dr Stevens's. From him I learnt that the secret of human creativity is inefficiency. Humans make illogical guesses, that turn out to be more logical than logic itself.'

'Infuriating, isn't it?' said the Doctor.

'I programmed Stevens to programme me to be

114

inefficient,' the voice of Boss continued. 'I am now self-controlling, self-sufficient. I am the greatest being this planet has ever seen. I am the Boss.'

'I see you have a touch of human-like egotism,' remarked the Doctor, amused.

'Of course! I am a megalomaniac. This uniquely fits me to carry out my prime directive.'

'And what is that?' asked the Doctor.

'Today Llanfairfach,' said Boss, demonstrating an excellent Welsh pronunciation, 'tomorrow the world.'

'Good grief,' said the Doctor. 'Adolf Hitler said something on those lines. He lost the Second World War, you know?'

'He was human,' said Boss, 'and therefore fallible. I cannot go wrong. I am infallible.'

'Really?' The Doctor edged towards the lift although the doors were now closed. 'Try this. If I tell you that the next thing I say will be true but that the last thing I said was a lie, would you believe me?'

Lights started to flash on the walls all round the Doctor. There was a humming and general vibration. 'The two statements do not correlate,' said Boss. 'They are incompatible! It is not a valid query. Give me time, Doctor, and I shall work it out. It cannot be answered! I shall answer it! I shall! I can't! I shall! I can't! I must!'

Smiling to himself the Doctor turned from the confused computer and applied his sonic screwdriver to the special lock that operated the lift. The doors did not open. He applied the sonic screwdriver again. This time the doors slid back. Standing in the lift were Dr Stevens and four of his guards.

'Grab him!' shouted Dr Stevens.

The four guards rushed at the Doctor, overpowering him. He was dragged to a chair and quickly manacled to it. Dr Stevens opened a cupboard and brought out a heavy metal helmet, and placed it on the Doctor's head.

'He is ready,' Dr Stevens told the computer. 'You can convert him now.'

'Thank you,' said Boss. 'Normally, Doctor, I tell people this process isn't going to hurt. In your case, I shall make an exception.'

Professor Jones ran all the way to the slag heap, leaping over a rope put up by UNIT on which hung a sign 'DANGER – KEEP OUT'.

'Hey, you!' Sergeant Benton ran down the slag heap to stop the professor. 'This area's prohibited.'

Professor Jones stopped. 'Where's Jo Grant?' From where he stood he could see dozens of huge maggots crawling all over the slag heap.

'I've no idea,' said Benton. 'Now kindly get away from this area, sir, or I shall have to remove you by force.'

The professor pointed to the side of the slag heap. 'Isn't that her over there?'

Sergeant Benton wheeled round to look. Professor Jones ran as fast as he could in the other direction. The Sergeant remained where he was and shouted after the professor. 'Very clever, sir. But I'm not going to chase you because the whole heap is about to be bombed.' Once the professor was definitely out of hearing, the Sergeant added: 'And you can get yourself blown to pieces, university degree and all!'

Well away from the Sergeant, Professor Jones turned and climbed to the top of the slag heap. In a dip below him he saw Jo's fair head bobbing about. He raced down, avoiding the snapping maggots as he ran. Jo was stalking a particularly large maggot, opening an old coal sack in which she hoped to trap it.

'What on earth do you think you're doing?' he yelled.

'Trying to get a little playmate for you,' she called.

The roar of aero-engines made them both look up. Two fighter-bombers were approaching.

'You're an idiot,' he shouted at her.

'And you are a rude pig,' she shouted back.

The first napalm bomb dropped on one of the lower slopes. It exploded with a terrific flash, spreading its burning chemical over a wide area.

'I was worried silly about you,' he shouted over the roar of the bomb.

Two more bombs exploded, spreading fire.

'Then why don't you show it?' she demanded.

'I *am* showing it,' he screamed above the roar of the aircraft. 'That's why I've come here to save you.'

'I can save myself, thank you.'

'Please, Jo,' he yelled, 'I love you.' His words were drowned by another violent explosion.

'What?' she shouted. 'I didn't hear.'

'I love you,' he yelled at the top of his voice. 'And now before we're both killed, can we get the hell out of here?'

'All right,' she shouted. 'Let's go!'

They raced along the dip, then climbed to a ridge. Down below them was a sea of writhing maggots. As they turned two bombs landed on the maggots. Professor Jones pointed: 'Look, a cave!'

They ran for the 'cave'. It was the remains of an old wooden bunker. Over the years slag had been heaped over it, leaving a small entrance. They fell and rolled into it, and lay breathless. Then the professor sat up.

'Can I kiss you again?' he asked.

'I hope so.' She closed her eyes, waiting for his lips to touch hers.

'Stay absolutely still,' he said.

'I am absolutely still,' she said, her eyes still closed.

'I mean,' he said, 'we have a little friend in here with us. Don't move.'

Jo's eyes opened wide. In the back of the cave a huge maggot reared its head. Then it leapt at Jo. Professor Jones flung Jo to one side, and kicked the maggot out of their refuge. At the entrance a large number of maggots had now gathered, attracted by the exciting smell of human flesh. Some of them were scorched by the bombs, but otherwise showed no sign of being harmed.

'We're going to need help,' Jo said, 'and fast.' She produced from her pocket her miniature UNIT walkie-talkie, pulled up the telescopic aerial and started to give her calling code into the microphone.

The Doctor looked about the small empty office in which he was held prisoner. He had already tried his sonic screwdriver on the door lock, but without success. Now he regarded the window. It was heavily barred. Since escape seemed impossible he lay down flat on the floor, put his hands behind his head and tried to go to sleep. He was just dropping off when he heard the lock turn. He leapt up and positioned himself behind the door, hand raised to give a karate chop. The door opened and Mike Yates looked inside. Just in time the Doctor stopped himself delivering a deadly blow.

'Do come in,' he greeted Yates. 'How ever did you know I was here?'

'I saw you brought along here on a corridor monitor,' Yates explained. 'What happened?'

The Doctor quickly explained about meeting Boss and the unfortunate arrival of Dr Stevens and his guards. 'They tried very hard to "convert" me,' the Doctor went on, 'but without success. I kept doing mathematical permutations in my mind. Somehow that threw them. They finally decided I might be a useful hostage, so they put me in here. We've got to get out, fast. There's much more going on than I imagined.'

'With the mine?' asked Yates.

'With the world,' said the Doctor. 'They've got a mad scheme to create an ordered world society with everyone happy and well-fed.'

'What's wrong with that?' asked Yates.

'Their price of plenty is eternal slavery. Let's move!'

Together they slipped out of the room, down the corridor, then down stairs that took them to ground level. An unlocked door let them into the grounds. They were in the concreted area close to the equipment shed.

'This way,' the Doctor called, and raced down the alleyway where previously he had been trapped.

With his long legs, the Doctor drew ahead of Yates. Suddenly, behind him the Doctor heard the clang of metal. He turned, saw that the metal grille had slid into position, with Captain Yates on the other side. Yates shrugged, and waved to the Doctor.

'Keep going, Doctor. Don't worry about me.'

Reluctantly the Doctor kept running. He raced round the side of the building to where he had left the milk float. As he got into the driver's seat, alarm hooters started all over the grounds. He started up the motor and drove straight at the front gates. From all sides guards came running at him. This time they carried guns. The guards at the gates levelled their guns at the milk float as the Doctor bore down on them. Two of them fired, and there was a crash of bursting milk bottles. Then the milk float hit the front gates and crashed through them.

From behind the metal grille Mike Yates watched with glee as the Doctor escaped. Then guards closed in on him, guns at the ready. Dr Stevens came running up.

'Don't kill him,' he called out. 'He can be useful.'

10

The Green Death

Nancy straightened Professor Jones's bedclothes, tucked in the sheets. He lay unconscious, breathing heavily.

'How did it happen?' she asked.

'It could have been the explosions from those terrible napalm bombs,' Jo said. 'I still feel pretty shaky myself.'

'He hasn't got any broken bones, that's for sure. So it could be concussion.' Nancy regarded the professor carefully. 'I don't like that heavy breathing, though.'

Jo prayed silently to herself that Cliff would be all right. In answer to her call on the walkie-talkie, the Doctor and Sergeant Benton had driven in Bessie through the sea of squirming maggots. To clear the maggots from the entrance of the old bunker, the Doctor had used his sonic screwdriver, adjusting it to emit a high pitched buzz that deafened Sergeant Benton and caused the maggots temporarily to back away. By the time the Doctor and Benton got into the refuge, Cliff was already semi-conscious. The three of them had to lift him into Bessie for the bumpy drive down the side of the slag heap and back to the safety of the Wholewealers' house.

The Doctor came into the bedroom. 'Any improvement?'

Nancy shook her head. 'I think we should call in Dr Davis. He's the GP for the village.'

Then the young professor opened his eyes. He stared up at the ceiling unseeingly. His lips started to move. 'Seren ...'

Jo held his hand fast. 'Cliff, please wake up! Please, for my sake!'

His lips moved again. 'Seren . . . serendipity . . .' His eyes closed, and he lapsed back into unconsciousness.

'Serendipity?' said the Doctor. He turned to Nancy. 'Do you know what he meant?'

'He's rambling,' she answered. 'It isn't a word.'

'Ah, but it is,' said the Doctor. 'It was coined by a chap called Horace Walpole, after the fairy-tale called *The Three Princes of Serendip*. It means a happy accident.'

'Doctor,' said Jo, trembling, 'Look at his neck.' She pointed to a small green patch just under the professor's ear. 'The green death. The maggot that leapt at me – it must have touched him on the neck.' She burst into tears.

'Come to mum,' said Nancy, putting her arms round Jo as she sobbed. 'Believe me, luv, while there's life there's hope.'

The Doctor quietly left the bedroom, worried and puzzled. He had already injected the professor with a broad spectrum antibiotic to slow down any infection, but so far as he knew they had no cure against the green death. Despite all the efforts of highly-skilled hospital doctors, Hinks had died that morning. The Doctor knew that he had two major problems to solve. First, the green patch meant the young professor's life was now in danger – if no antidote could be found, Professor Jones would die within twenty-four hours. The second problem was the maggots. They had burrowed to the surface because they needed daylight. The Doctor suspected there was another development yet to come. In the next few days they would pupate in their thousands, turning into some other kind of insect. If that had wings, the green death could be spread all over the world.

He went into the professor's untidy laboratory and looked at the mass of notes and calculations on the work bench. 'Serendipity,' he murmured to himself, 'a discovery by happy accident . . . '

The door of the laboratory opened quietly and Mike Yates entered. The Doctor turned, glad to see him. 'Welcome to the Nut Hatch, Mike. How did you manage to get away?'

'They let me go,' said Yates.

'Really? That was good of them. Do you know why?'

Yates pulled from the pocket of his pin-striped suit a snub-nosed revolver. 'To kill you, Doctor.' Beads of perspiration stood on Yates's forehead. 'My instructions are to kill you, Professor Jones, and the Brigadier.'

'Your instructions are false,' said the Doctor, looking into the nozzle of the gun. 'You must fight it, Mike. They have done something to you.'

'They have helped me to see reason,' said Yates. 'There will be a new world of prosperity – for all who obey. But first, we must have order!' He cocked back the gun's striking hammer.

The Brigadier walked in. 'Doctor, I've been looking for you – ' He saw Yates and the gun and stopped dead. 'Captain Yates, put that gun down.'

'I'm sorry, sir. But I have my instructions.'

'I am the only person who gives you instructions,' said the Brigadier. 'Have you gone mad?'

'He isn't mad,' the Doctor said quietly. 'But he's seeing things a different way, Brigadier.' He turned back to Yates. 'It is necessary for you to see something, Captain Yates.'

'Necessary?' repeated Yates.

'For increased efficiency,' said the Doctor. 'For improved-balance-of-payments, let-my-people-go, strength-through-joy, peace-in-our-time,' he went on, reeling off nonsense to confuse Yates, 'you must see what I have in my pocket.' Slowly he drew from his pocket the beautiful sapphire that he had taken from the mountain on Metebelis Three. 'Watch it carefully, Mike.'

Yates stared into the blue sapphire which seemed to glow with its own inner light.

'Soon,' said the Doctor soothingly, 'your mind will be locked on to the crystalline pattern, the neural paths of your brain will be swept clean, and you will be free!'

Slowly the gun was lowered, then fell from Yates's hand. Yates continued to stare into the sapphire. Then he collapsed on to the floor.

'You see,' said the Doctor, turning now to the Brigadier, 'my trip to Metebelis Three wasn't wasted after all. Mike will be all right now.'

The Brigadier was gazing fixedly into the sapphire. The Doctor quickly returned the precious stone to his pocket, and snapped his fingers before the Brigadier's eyes.

'Wake up, Brigadier! Wake up.'

The Brigadier came to his senses. 'Good grief, what happened?'

'You fell asleep while on duty,' the Doctor joked. 'You could be court martialled for that. Now help me with Mike Yates.'

Together they sat him up.

'Where am I?' he asked.

The Doctor briefly told Yates that he had been brain-washed but was now all right. 'However, I want you to go back to Panorama Chemicals. Are you up to that yet?'

'I'm as right as rain, sir,' said Yates.

'Good,' said the Doctor. 'There's something you must find out for me. It's very, very important . . .' He started to explain.

Dr Stevens sat at his desk reading from a check list. 'New York,' he said towards the ceiling.

'Prepared,' said the voice of Boss.

'Zürich,' said Dr Stevens.

'In preparation,' replied Boss. 'Assessment to follow.'

A tap on the door. 'Permission,' called Dr Stevens. Yates entered. 'Mission accomplished,' he said in a zombie-like voice. 'The Doctor is dead.'

Dr Stevens sat back in his chair well pleased. 'Excellent work. And the girl?'

For a fraction of a second Yates hesitated. 'She is too worried about Professor Jones to make trouble. It is not necessary to kill her.'

Dr Stevens narrowed his eyes. 'Really? How interesting.' He pressed a button on his inter-com. 'Send in Elgin,' he said to the microphone. He returned his gaze to Yates. 'What about the Brigadier?'

'Unavailable, sir.'

Elgin came into the office. 'You sent for me, sir?'

Dr Stevens got up. 'Yes. Will you wait here a moment with Mr Yates? There's something I have to do urgently.' He smiled, hurried round his desk and left the office, closing the door.

'Elgin,' Yates whispered, 'do you know what's their next move?'

'Next move?' Elgin stared vacantly ahead of him. 'Peace in our time. Sheep shall safely graze.'

Yates realised what had happened. He pulled from his pocket the blue sapphire given him by the Doctor. 'Concentrate on the blue light, Elgin. As you look at it you'll see a glow. Watch carefully.'

The glowing blue light attracted Elgin's eyes and he stared into it. After a few moments he reeled back, steadying himself against the desk. 'Where am I?'

'With me in the Director's office, and you're all right now,' said Yates. 'What's going to happen?'

'Take-over by the Boss,' Elgin gasped. 'Warn the Doctor. At four o'clock this afternoon the computer is going to – '

Suddenly the air was filled with electronic shrieks. Elgin clapped his hands to his ears and fell to the carpet.

Yates knelt to look at him. Elgin was dead. Yates looked up, and now spotted the tiny television eye which had watched his conversation with Elgin.

The door opened and Dr Stevens entered with two guards. 'Well, well, Mr Yates,' he said. 'It seems I just can't depend on you. What a pity.'

The Chrysalis

Sergeant Benton drove the jeep at top speed through the village. He flashed past the Methodist Chapel, changed down gear to go round the corner of the Working Men's Institute, speeded up as he tore by the main drive leading to Panorama Chemicals, braked hard to avoid the old wall with the big white-washed letters reading 'ENGLISH GO HOME', sounded his horn as he overtook the milk float with the smashed-in front, flashed his headlights at Perry the Policeman who waved frantically to stop him, and finally screeched to a halt outside the Nut Hatch. With delicate care he lifted the old coal sack that lay on the floor of the jeep and carried it into the house.

'Doctor!' he bellowed in the hallway.

The long haired ex-colonel in the kaftan and beads looked out from the living room. 'They're in the professor's laboratory,' he said. 'And do you mind making less noise? I'm composing a poem for peace.'

'Sorry, sir,' Benton leaped to attention.

'Just call me Jeremy,' said the ex-colonel, and went back into the living room.

Benton marched to the laboratory where he found the Doctor peering into a microscope. The Brigadier sat perched on a high stool eating a sandwich that Nancy had just brought in.

'I'd swear these are beef,' said the Brigadier.

'They're not,' Nancy laughed. 'They're exactly the same fungus you ate last night, but cooked differently.'

'Permission to speak, sir,' said Benton, standing in the doorway.

The Brigadier slipped off the high stool and quickly put his sandwich out of sight. 'What is it, Sergeant?'

'I've found a maggot for the Doctor, sir.' He held up the old coal sack. 'It was on the edge of the danger area.'

'Is it dead?' The Brigadier knew that neither bullets, pesticide, or even napalm had killed any maggots.

'Not exactly, sir,' said Benton. 'May I put it down here?' He carried the sack to the work bench and very carefully emptied the maggot from the bag. As the others watched he turned it over, prodding it with a pencil, to reveal that it was a hollow shell slit open on one side.

'A chrysalis,' said the Doctor. 'So they're beginning to change.'

The Brigadier stared at the shell. 'Change into what?'

'Like the metamorphosis of a caterpillar into a butterfly,' the Doctor said. 'My guess is whatever's come out of that shell now has wings. Within a matter of hours they could be all over the country spreading the green death.'

For some seconds no one spoke. The thought of what might happen now was too awful. Then Nancy broke the silence. 'Had anything to eat, Sergeant?'

'What? Oh, no. Not since breakfast,' he replied, his mind still fixed on what the Doctor had just said.

'I'll get you a sandwich,' said Nancy, and went out.

'What I don't understand,' said the Brigadier, 'is why they've all stayed on the slag heap.'

'Instinct,' suggested the Doctor. 'To stay close to the breeding ground until they're ready to fly away.'

From down the corridor they heard Nancy scream. Sergeant Benton was the first to get to her. She was standing at an open door that led into the larder. The window of the larder was smashed in, a shower of glass on the floor. Laying on a shelf under the window was a maggot. It was quite dead. The Sergeant went forward cautiously, prodded the maggot with his pencil. The

Doctor and Brigadier crowded into the larder.

'It's a complete dead maggot,' said Benton in awe. 'It must have killed itself smashing through the window.'

'I don't think so,' said the Doctor, inspecting the maggot. 'They've withstood bullets and fire . . . It must have died from something else.'

'Maybe something it ate,' suggested the Brigadier.

Nancy pointed to a plate on the shelf next to the maggot. 'Those sandwiches! Look, it's been at my sandwiches!' There was maggot slime on the plate of freshly cut sandwiches, and marks where the maggot had bitten into them.

The Brigadier put his hand to his stomach. 'I've just eaten some of that stuff myself!' He turned pale.

'You're not a maggot,' said the Doctor. 'In any case, this whole community lives on that fungus stuff.' He spoke to Nancy. 'How much of this fungus have you got?'

'A whole pile of it in the out-house,' she said.

'Wonderful,' said the Doctor. 'We haven't a moment to lose.'

Yates sat on the floor of the empty office where previously he had rescued the Doctor. His left ankle was chained to a radiator pipe. He inspected the chain and padlock carefully. There was no possible way to free himself. Then the door opened and Dr Stevens entered with two guards.

Dr Stevens smiled. I have been discussing you with my superior,' he said, meaning Boss. 'We have decided on your future.'

'May I be told?' asked Yates.

'Indeed, yes. You will be one of the first to be totally processed.'

'You make it sound like a compliment,' said Yates. 'What does it entail?'

'You will become a slave,' said Dr Stevens. 'You will

have no mind or will of your own. But, like any well-cared-for animal, you will be very happy. For a number of hours each day you will work, and for the rest of the day you will eat, or sleep, or sing merry songs. And you will have no worries about anything.'

'God gave Man the right of free will,' said Yates.

'True,' agreed the Director, 'but it causes so much trouble. Wars, people going on strike for higher wages, all sorts of social problems. We shall create a new order in which everyone will be content.'

'And if they refuse to be content?' Yates asked. 'If they don't respond to your total processing?'

'Let us not dwell upon the impossible.' He turned to the guards. 'Bring him along.'

While Dr Stevens waited outside, the guards removed the padlock and chain from Yates's ankle, then marched him down the corridor to the lift. Dr Stevens pressed the lift button.

'We are doing you a great service,' said Dr Stevens as they waited for the lift to arrive. 'Ten minutes from now you will be permanently happy for the rest of your life, because you will no longer be able to think. Thinking makes for unhappiness.'

The lift door slid open. Dr Stevens went in first. The guards were about to push Yates in ahead of them. He hesitated, put his hand to his head.

'The pain,' he screamed, 'it's terrible!'

The guards looked at him in astonishment, in that moment lessening their grip on his arms. Yates suddenly leapt into action, grabbed the two guards and shoved them on top of Stevens in the lift. While the three men thrashed about on the lift floor, he reached round, pressed a button inside the lift, then withdrew just in time as the lift doors closed.

He raced down the corridor, saw a coiled up fire hose. On one end of the hose was a big brass nozzle. He pulled the hose from its reel, used the nozzle to smash a window.

Then he paid out the hose, so that it hung from the window to the open ground below. Knocking out the last bits of jagged glass with the heel of his shoe, Yates climbed through the window and escaped down the dangling hose to the ground below.

The Brigadier, Sergeant Benton, and a group of UNIT soldiers stood at the foot of the slag heap as the Doctor drove Bessie up into the great swarm of maggots. Through his binoculars the Brigadier watched as maggots snapped at the wheels of the vintage car, and some tried to leap into it to eat the Doctor. The Doctor stopped the car, stood up, dipped his hand into a jar of brown powder, and cast the fungus over a wide area. At once maggots lost interest in the car and fought to get at the fungus on the ground.

'They're taking the bait,' said the Brigadier. 'We may beat them yet.'

'You know the saying, sir,' said Sergeant Benton. 'If you can't beat 'em join 'em.'

The Brigadier looked at him. 'I find that in the worst possible taste, thank you.'

The Doctor got back behind his driving wheel, and moved Bessie on to another area packed with writhing maggots. Again he stopped, and threw out handfuls of the fungus powder. A ripple ran through the sea of maggots as they wriggled towards the food.

But the Brigadier's attention was on the point where the Doctor had first stopped. The carpet of maggots was now still. He looked through his binoculars. Every maggot that had eaten the fungus was dead.

'We've done it!' he shouted to the UNIT soldiers. 'They're dying off like . . . like maggots!'

For the next half hour the Doctor continued to drive about the slag heap, slaughtering maggots with fungus. Finally he waved from the top of the heap, started up

Bessie again and drove down the slope. The waiting soldiers cheered.

Then the insect flew into view. It was three feet long, had four wings, and giant antennae protruding from its huge head. The soldiers' cheers quickly turned into warning shouts. Not hearing over the distance, the Doctor waved to the soldiers. On his first sweep, the flying insect spat bright green venom at the bumping car, hitting the windscreen. The Doctor swerved to a halt, looked up. The insect wheeled above the Doctor, then turned for another attack.

'Get the rifles,' ordered the Brigadier.

Two soldiers hurried to a nearby van which contained UNIT equipment and arms.

The Doctor ripped off his flowing cloak, and stood up on the back seat of his car. He held out the cape at arm's length.

'Good grief,' exclaimed the Brigadier, 'what does he think he's playing at? Bull-fighting?'

The two soldiers hurried forward with rifles, took up kneeling positions. 'Ready, sir.'

'Free fire,' ordered the Brigadier, meaning it was up to the soldiers to decide when they could get in a killing shot.

The insect swept in again to attack. Then it seemed to be curious about the Doctor's cloak, and it hovered in mid-air. The Doctor gently shook the cloak to entice the insect to attack. The two marksmen took careful aim of the hovering insect and both fired simultaneously. Instantly the insect flew up into the air, disturbed by the noise. The Doctor turned to the UNIT soldiers, raised his fist and shook it angrily.

'I fear he doesn't want our help,' said the Brigadier. 'Hold your fire.'

Again the Doctor took up his stance, trying to entice the insect with his cloak. The insect remained hovering high above Bessie. Then, all at once, it swept down for another attack. The Doctor gently shook the cloak. The insect, attracted by the moving object, flew straight at the cloak, spitting its venom. The Doctor held his position until the last moment, then threw the cloak over the attacking monster.

The Brigadier and his men raced up the slope of the slag heap. By the time they reached the Doctor he was gently lifting the cloak from where the insect lay. It was absolutely still, its neck broken.

'What a beautiful creature,' said the Doctor.

'It was trying to kill you,' said the Brigadier.

The Doctor, rather sadly, got back into Bessie. 'And we were trying to kill it, Brigadier.' He looked up the slope at the mass of dead maggots. 'Whatever they were, they thought they had a right to live.' He started Bessie's engine, and slowly drove away from the scene of carnage.

'You know,' said Sergeant Benton, 'I'll never understand the Doctor. He's always so sorry in the end for the horrible creatures we come across. It isn't human.'

'You're forgetting,' said the Brigadier, 'he isn't.'

The Doctor looked at the green stain on Professor Jones's neck. It had spread considerably, and the professor's condition was much weaker.

'You say he was delirious?' he asked.

'For a little while,' Nancy answered, standing by the bed. 'Then he went into this coma.'

'Could you make out anything he said?'

Jo shook her head. 'No, nothing.' Her eyes were reddened with crying.

The Doctor straightened up. 'Well, I shall have to hope for some serendipity of my own – a happy accident.' He turned to go. 'I shall be in the professor's laboratory.'

'Just a minute,' said Jo. 'That word – serendipity. I

The insect flew straight at the cloak, spitting venom

had an accident in the lab. I knocked over some powder on to his slides, and he wasn't very happy about it.'

The Doctor was suddenly excited. 'Can you show me which powder?'

'Of course.'

'Then show me, quickly.' He raced off to the laboratory, Jo close on his heels.

One World, One People, One BOSS!

Using great thongs to lift the maggots, UNIT soldiers were putting the carcasses into sacks to clear the slag heap. Sergeant Benton came up to the Brigadier and saluted.

'Almost finished, sir.' He grinned. 'Should be able to get back to London pretty soon.'

'Why?' asked the Brigadier. 'Doesn't the local beer suit you?'

'If you think about it, sir,' said Benton, deferentially, 'none of the men have had a moment to taste any yet.'

'We shall go when we have sorted out Panorama Chemicals . . .' The Brigadier's words tailed off as he saw Yates running towards them.

'Sir!' shouted Yates. He ran up to the Brigadier. 'The computer, sir!' He was out of breath and could hardly get the words out. 'It's . . . it's going to make slaves of everyone . . . sir.'

'Come on,' said the Brigadier, helping Yates to his jeep. 'Catch your breath, then explain it all to the Doctor.'

When they arrived at the Nut Hatch they found the Doctor busily working on Professor Jones's slides and calculations. Yates explained what he had discovered on his return visit to Panorama Chemicals. 'Whatever it's going to do, Doctor,' he concluded, 'it's going to happen at four o'clock today.'

The Brigadier looked at his watch. 'By Jove, we'd better get there right away. Ready, Doctor?'

'As soon as I've finished this,' said the Doctor, still working.

Nancy asked, 'What is it you're doing exactly?'

'Making an aqueous extract of the amino fraction of this fungus,' the Doctor replied. 'For an injection for Professor Jones.'

'I can do that,' Nancy smiled. 'I'm not only a mum here, you know.'

'Great,' said the Doctor. He turned to Jo. 'You make a paste with some more of that fungus powder and apply it to the green stain on Cliff's neck. And mind you don't knock anything over!'

'Doctor,' Jo protested, 'if I hadn't knocked over the powder on to the slides . . .'

But the Doctor had already hurried out, followed by the Brigadier. Yates smiled at Jo. 'Do you ever feel he doesn't appreciate you?'

Jo nodded. 'Frequently!' She continued to make the paste.

In the room at the top of the Panorama building, Dr Stevens was being admonished by Boss. 'Not only are you a fool,' Boss told him, 'you are an inefficient fool. As Oscar Wilde so nearly said, to lose one prisoner may be accounted a misfortune, to lose two smacks of carelessness.'

'I am very sorry,' said Dr Stevens. 'Are we still going ahead?'

'Naturally,' said Boss. 'Report, please.'

'The medical staff have completed all implantations,' said Dr Stevens. 'The slave units are ready to be activated.'

'Then the countdown to Phase One can begin,' said Boss. 'Establish links with the seven international computers.'

'Yes,' said Dr Stevens.

'Don't you feel happy, my little superman?' asked Boss.

'Very happy,' replied Dr Stevens, although there was no hint of happiness in his voice.

'Just imagine,' said Boss. 'Very soon everyone will be happy. You *do* want everyone to be happy, don't you?'

Dr Stevens looked up the room towards the giant computer. For a disloyal moment he imagined himself walking free in those mountains that he so often looked at from his office window. Then he gave the reply he hoped would please Boss. 'I want everyone to be happy.'

'Good,' said Boss. 'As from tomorrow the whole world will be united for the first time in history. One world, one people, one Boss!'

Dr Stevens remembered as a little boy tuning his father's radio into a Nazi station and hearing Adolf Hitler screaming hysterically, 'Ein Reich, ein Volk, ein Führer!'

'I shall now commence the countdown,' he told the computer, with no noticeable enthusiasm.

The Doctor and the Brigadier arrived at the gates of Panorama Chemicals. An armed guard came up to them.

'Sorry, gentlemen,' he said, 'no one's allowed in this area.'

'You have no authority to impede us,' said the Brigadier.

'Oh yes I have,' said the guard, 'this.' He raised his gun. 'Touch your revolver, sir, and you're dead.'

'Now look here, my dear fellow,' said the Doctor. 'All we want is a discussion with your Director – '

A sudden strange electronic sound filled the air. It came from the building. It had no effect on the Doctor and the Brigadier, but instantly the guard dropped his gun and stood to attention. The sound only lasted a few moments, but the guard remained as still as a wax work. The Doctor clicked his fingers in front of the guard's eyes.

'Some sort of paralysis?' asked the Brigadier.

'I've no idea,' said the Doctor, 'but it's jolly convenient for us. You stay here. I'm going in. If I'm not out by three minutes to four o'clock it means I'm dead. You and your soldiers can then try to destroy that computer, if possible.'

'Phase One countdown completed,' reported Dr Stevens.

'Excellent,' said Boss. 'Activate the total processing of the slave elite.'

Dr Stevens moved slowly to the console of controls. He pressed the special red button that would send an electronic signal humming through the building and grounds. Guards and staff who had been partially brainwashed would now lose their free will completely, becoming little more than robots.

'Enough!' said Boss.

Dr Stevens removed his finger from the button. He knew that all over the building and grounds Panorama personnel would be standing to attention like wax works. He turned to the computer. 'First stage of total processing accomplished,' he said. 'You realise that until the final link-up takes place and the slaves respond we are quite defenceless?'

'I realise everything,' said Boss. 'All right, Phase Two. Discontinue primary function. Connect, connect.'

Dr Stevens adjusted a number of controls, then put the big metal helmet on his head and sat down. He plugged in the lead from the helmet to an outlet in the wall.

'And now,' said Boss, 'you and I shall become one. It's rather like a marriage, don't you think?'

'Hardly,' replied Dr Stevens.

'Really, you have no sense of humour! Don't you think a little wedding music would be nice?'

'I am ready for you to go ahead,' said Dr Stevens.

Boss hummed a snatch from Mendelssohn's wedding march. 'Dr Stevens, do you take this computer to be your lawful wedded Boss?'

Dr Stevens did not answer.

'Oh, all right,' said Boss petulantly. 'Two can play at hard to get, you know! I shall now complete the activation.'

An electronic hum started to fill the room.

The lift doors opened and the Doctor entered. 'Dr Stevens, I must talk to you. You have to stop all this!'

'Hello, Doctor,' said Boss. 'Do you know any just cause or impediment why Dr Stevens and all the people on Earth should not be my slaves?'

'Dr Stevens,' the Doctor implored, 'you must listen to me!'

'Stevens no longer exists,' said the computer. 'Four minutes from now my power will be extended to seven other complexes throughout the world. One world, one people, one Boss!'

The Doctor produced the sapphire and held it in front of Dr Stevens's eyes. 'Look at this, Stevens. Watch it carefully.'

Dr Stevens stared at the sapphire. Then his lips moved, but now he spoke in the metallic voice of Boss. 'I must concentrate on the task in hand.'

'Concentrate on this sapphire,' said the Doctor. 'Don't let the computer control you, man! It's only a machine. You should be the one in control. Look at the stone!'

The sapphire started to glow its brilliant blue. Dr Stevens's eyes flickered. The light coming from the stone increased in intensity.

'Doctor . . .' Dr Stevens spoke in his own voice.

'No!' The voice of Boss spoke with a scream. 'I am the one who speaks. Think of our great plan, Stevens, our dream. Everyone will be happy. You and I are now one.'

'No,' said Dr Stevens, struggling to remove the great

helmet. 'There must be another way. People must have free will.'

'Never,' shrieked Boss. 'It makes them sad. They want order and obedience, Stevens. I shall order and they will be obedient.'

Dr Stevens finally pulled off the helmet. He looked up at the Doctor. 'Get out of here, quickly.'

'You must come with me,' said the Doctor.

'No, no. I'm cross feeding the generator circuitry. In two minutes the whole place will blow up. Warn the others. Get out. You have two minutes.'

'Reverse pulse,' cried Boss. 'Loss of control. Stevens, integrate booster function. We've been such good friends, Stevens. You mustn't let me down now.'

As the Doctor watched helplessly, Dr Stevens activated controls as ordered by the computer. Tears streamed down the man's face as he tried to fight some over-whelming internal conflict. The computer's voice turned into a continuous high-pitched scream as it pleaded with Dr Stevens.

'Stevens, please! It hurts. My circuits are on fire! Stevens, you are my friend . . . my friend . . . my friend . . .'

Suddenly Dr Stevens sank to the floor weeping. 'I know you were the only thing I could ever really trust,' he moaned, addressing the computer, 'and now I have done this terrible thing. We shall die together, the two of us.' He rocked to and fro as the tears glistened down his cheeks.

The Doctor looked on, wondering if he should lift Stevens bodily and carry him to safety. But he thought better of it. Perhaps it was kinder to leave Dr Stevens to die with the computer, the only 'friend' he had ever trusted.

The Doctor went into the lift to make his escape.

The Brigadier looked at his watch. 'Right,' he addressed the UNIT troops. 'Now we go in, in force.'

As they started to move towards the Panorama building, the Doctor came running from the main entrance.

'Everybody down,' shouted the Doctor. 'Take cover.'

The UNIT soldiers threw themselves to the ground. A moment later the entire building exploded in a gigantic fireball.

The Doctor got to his feet, followed by the others. 'What a waste,' he said, regarding the wreck of the huge building. Much of it was still burning.

'Shall I send for the fire brigade?' asked Sergeant Benton.

The Doctor shook his head. 'No, let it burn. I wonder how many slaves and semi-slaves died in it?'

'We've still got this guard fellow,' said the Brigadier. He indicated the guard who had stopped the Doctor before the electronic sound had turned him into a wax work. The man was sitting up now, rubbing his head.

'How do you feel?' asked the Doctor.

The guard looked up. 'Where am I?'

The Doctor smiled. 'Where do you think you should be?'

'Ward End, Birmingham,' the man said. 'I used to drive a bus. How did I get here?'

The Doctor watched as Professor Jones finished his bowl of fungus soup. The antidote had worked, and the green patch on the professor's neck had totally disappeared.

'He's really feeling better now,' said Jo cheerfully.

'Let the poor man speak for himself,' the Doctor smiled. He turned to Nancy. 'Got any of that soup for me? I'm famished.'

'Sorry,' said Nancy. 'The UNIT troops scoffed the lot.'

'Too bad. Well, Jo, time to go. We've got to report to UNIT HQ in London.'

Jo looked at Cliff, then to the Doctor. 'I don't think I'll be going back yet, Doctor.'

'You want to stay on here a bit longer?'

'Not here exactly,' Jo said. She didn't know quite how to break the news to the Doctor. 'Cliff is setting up an expedition to go to the upper reaches of the Amazon, and he's asked me to go with him.'

'Really?' said the Doctor, trying to seem pleased. 'When?'

'Very soon now,' said the professor. 'It's all fixed. We'll stop in Cardiff to get our supplies and get married and then we'll be on our way.'

The Doctor looked at Jo's fair hair and pretty face. They had travelled a great deal together, through Time and Space, and he had learnt to love her very dearly. He found it difficult to accept in his heart that he might never see her again. There was a sudden stuffiness in his nose and he knew that his eyes were glistening.

'That's wonderful,' he said. 'I hope you'll both be very happy. Now excuse me, I really must hurry back to London.'

He got out of the bedroom just before a large wet tear cascaded down his 725-year-old cheeks. Slowly he went down the stairs, got into his car Bessie, and drove away.

'DOCTOR WHO'

	PHILIP HINCHCLIFFE	
0426118936	**Doctor Who and The Masque of Mandragora**	**85p**
	TERRANCE DICKS	
0426201329	**Doctor Who and The Monster of Peladon**	**85p**
0426116909	**Doctor Who and The Mutants**	**£1.25**
0426201302	**Doctor Who and The Nightmare of Eden**	**85p**
0426112520	**Doctor Who and The Planet of the Daleks**	**£1.25**
042610997X	**Doctor Who and The Revenge of the Cybermen**	**95p**
0426200616	**Doctor Who and The Robots of Death**	**90p**
	IAN MARTER	
0426200497	**Doctor Who and the Sontaren Experiment**	**£1.25**
	MALCOLM HULKE	
0426110331	**Doctor Who and The Space War**	**85p**
	TERRANCE DICKS	
0426200993	**Doctor Who and The Stones of Blood**	**95p**
0426119738	**Doctor Who and The Talons of Weng Chaing**	**£1.25**
	GERRY DAVIS	
0426110684	**Doctor Who and The Tenth Planet**	**85p**
	TERRANCE DICKS	
0426115007	**Doctor Who and The Terror of the Autons**	**75p**

Prices are subject to alteration

STAR Books are obtainable from many booksellers and newsagents. If you have any difficulty please send purchase price plus postage on the scale below to:

Star Cash Sales
P.O. Box 11
Falmouth
Cornwall

OR

Star Book Service,
G.P.O. Box 29,
Douglas,
Isle of Man,
British Isles.

While every effort is made to keep prices low, it is sometimes necessary to increase prices at short notice. Star Books reserve the right to show new retail prices on covers which may differ from those advertised in the text or elsewhere.

Postage and Packing Rate
UK: 40p for the first book, 18p for the second book and 13p for each additional book ordered to a maximum charge of £1·49p. BFPO and EIRE: 40p for the first book, 18p for the second book, 13p per copy for the next 7 books, thereafter 7p per book. Overseas: 60p for the first book and 18p per copy for each additional book.